The Lovers

The Lovers

A NOVEL

PAOLO COGNETTI

Translated from the Italian by Stash Luczkiw

HARPERVIA
An Imprint of HarperCollinsPublishers

Excerpt from *Arctic Dreams: Imagination and Desire in a Northern Landscape* by Barry Holstun Lopez (New York: Scribner's, 1986). Copyright ©1986 by Barry Holstun Lopez. Reprinted by permission of SLL/ Sterling Lord Literistic, Inc.

HarperCollins books may be purchased for educational, business, or sales promotional use. For information, please email the Special Markets Department at SPsales@harpercollins.com.

Italian language edition published as *La felicità del lupo* in Italy in 2021 by Giulio Einaudi editore s.p.a., Torino.

FIRST HARPERVIA EDITION PUBLISHED IN 2022

Designed by SBI Book Arts, LLC

Library of Congress Cataloging-in-Publication Data has been applied for.

ISBN 978-0-06-311540-8

22 23 24 25 26 LSC 10 9 8 7 6 5 4 3 2 1

As I traveled, I came to believe that people's desires and aspirations were as much a part of the land as the wind, solitary animals, and the bright fields of stone and tundra. And, too, that the land itself existed quite apart from these.

—Barry Lopez, *Arctic Dreams*

Contents

CONTENTS

The Lovers

1

A Little Restaurant

Fausto was forty years old when he took refuge in Fontana Fredda, looking for a place to start over. He had known those mountains since he was a boy, and his unhappiness when he was away from them was among the causes, or perhaps *the* cause, of the problems with the woman who almost became his wife. After the separation he rented a place up there and spent a September, an October, and a November walking the trails, gathering wood in the forest, and having dinner in front of the woodstove, savoring the salt of freedom and chewing the bitterness of solitude. He also wrote, or at least tried. In the autumn he saw the herds leave the mountain pastures, the larch needles turn yellow and fall, until the first snows, when despite having reduced his needs to the bone, the money he had put aside ran out. Winter presented him with the bill of a difficult year. There was someone he could ask for a job in Milan, but it would mean going down there, picking up the phone, settling the unfinished business with his ex. Then one evening, just before resigning himself to doing just that, he happened to open up before a glass of wine, in Fontana Fredda's only meeting place.

From behind her counter Babette understood perfectly. She had also come from the city, and she still had the accent as well as a certain elegance, though who knows when and how she got there. At some point she had taken over a restaurant in a place that offered no clientele between seasons apart from construction workers and cowherds, and she had christened it Babette's Feast. From then on everyone called her that, no one remembered her name from before. Fausto made friends with her because he had read Karen Blixen and picked up on the reference: the Babette of the story was a revolutionary who, after the Paris Commune had failed, wound up working as a cook in a Norwegian village full of bumpkins. This other Babette may not have served turtle soups, but she tended to take in strays and seek practical solutions to existential problems. After listening to him she asked: Do you know how to cook?

So at Christmas he was still there, wielding pots and pans amid the kitchen's smoke. There was also a ski slope in Fontana Fredda; every summer there was talk of closing it and every winter it somehow reopened. With a sign down at the crossroads and a little artificial snow blown across the pastures, it attracted families of skiers, and for three months a year transformed the mountain men into chairlift operators, snowmakers, snowcat drivers, and rescuers in a collective masquerade that he now took part in, too. The other cook was a veteran. In a few days she taught him how to degrease kilos of sausage, stop the pasta from overcooking with cold water, stretch the oil in the deep fryer, and how stirring the polenta for hours was a waste of effort, you just let it simmer there on a low flame and it would cook by itself.

Fausto liked being in the kitchen, but something else began to attract his attention. He had a small window through which he would pass the plates into the dining room and watch Silvia, the new waitress, take orders and serve the tables. Who knows where Babette had found her. She was not the kind of girl you would expect to find among the mountain men: young, cheerful, with the air of a world traveler. The sight of her carrying polenta and sausages seemed a sign of the times, like the flowers blossoming out of season, or the wolves that were said to have returned to the woods. Between Christmas and Epiphany they worked tirelessly, twelve hours a day, seven days a week, and they courted each other with her hanging orders for him on the corkboard, and him ringing the bell when the dishes were ready. They kidded each other:

two plain pastas, the *chef*'s special. Plain pasta is *off the menu*, he said. The dishes and skiers came and went with such speed that Fausto was there scouring the pots when he realized it was dark outside. Then he stopped for a moment, the mountains came back to his mind: he wondered if the wind had been blowing or if it had snowed up above and what the light had been like up there on the wide sun-drenched plateaus above the tree line, and if the lakes now looked like slabs of ice or soft, snowy basins. At eighteen hundred meters it was a strange beginning to the winter, with rain and snow, and in the morning, rain melting the overnight sleet.

Then one evening, after the holidays, with the floors damp and the dishes dried and stacked, he undid his cook's apron and came out for a drink. The bar at that hour slipped into a mode in which it quietly ran itself. Babette put on some music, left a bottle of grappa on the counter, and the snowcat operators came in to look for company between one pass over the slopes and the next, leveling the holes and bumps made by the skiers, hauling the pushed-down snow back up, and milling it where it was frozen to make it granular, up and down on their treads for long, dark hours. Silvia had a small room above the kitchen. Around eleven o'clock, from the bar, Fausto saw her come down with a towel around her head and drag a chair up to the woodstove to read a big book in the warmth. He was struck by the thought that she had just gotten out of the shower.

In the meantime he listened to the chatter of this snowcat driver they called Santorso, like the patron Saint Ursus of Aosta and the grappa distillery. Santorso was talking to him about grouse hunting and the snow. About how the snow was late that year, the snow so precious for protecting the burrows from frost, and about the problems a winter without snow gave to partridge and black grouse, and Fausto liked learning so many things he didn't know, but he wouldn't even think of losing sight of his waitress. At one point Silvia took the towel off her head and started combing her hair with her fingers, bringing it closer to the stove. Her hair was long, black, and straight, and there was a lot of intimacy in the way she combed it. Until she felt she was being watched. She looked up from her book and smiled at him with her fingers in her hair. The grappa burned Fausto's throat like a boy's first drink. Shortly after, the snowcats returned to work and Babette said good night to those two, reminded one or the other to put the croissants in the oven early in the morning, took the garbage bags away, and went home. She was happy to leave the keys, liquor, and music there, so her restaurant could encourage friendships even when she was gone, a little Paris Commune amid the Norwegian ice.

2

The Lovers

That evening she was the one who took him upstairs. If it were up to him they would have first had to wait for the thaw. The only heat in Silvia's room was what came from the kitchen, so the ritual of undressing was a bit rushed, but for Fausto, slipping into bed nude, next to an equally nude and trembling girl, had something moving and marvelous about it. He had been with the same woman for ten years, and for six months with his own insipid company. Exploring that body was like finally having a guest: he discovered that it was a strong, solid body below, sturdy thighs, skin smooth and taut; above, it was spiky with bones, little breasts, full of ribs, clavicles, elbows, and then cheekbones and teeth that would collide with him when Silvia got a bit rough. He

THE LOVERS

no longer remembered the patience it took to understand another person's tastes and make them understand his. But it was offset by his hands full of burns, cuts, detergent abrasions, and scars from the damn slicer, and in the end he found a certain correspondence in caressing her with them.

What a nice smell you have, he said. Like wood smoke.

You smell like grappa.

Does it bother you?

No, I like it. Grappa and resin. What is it?

It's the pine cones we put in the grappa.

You put pine cones in grappa?

Yeah, stone pine. We gather them in July.

Then you smell like July.

Fausto liked that idea, it was his favorite month. The thick and shady woods, the smell of hay in the fields, the gurgling streams, and the last snow up above, beyond the screes. He gave her a July kiss on that beautifully protruding clavicle.

I like your bones.

I'm glad. I've been carrying them around with me for twenty-seven years.

Twenty-seven? They've got a lot of mileage.

Yeah, we've been around the block.

So tell me. Let's hear where your bones were, say, at nineteen.

At nineteen I was in Bologna, studying art.

You're an artist?

No. At least that's what I figured out. That I'm not an artist, I mean. I was better at partying.

In Bologna, I can believe it. You hungry?

A bit.

Should I go get something?

Yeah, but only if it's quick, I'm cold already.

Back in a flash.

Fausto went down to the kitchen, looked through the refrigerators, passed the small window at the back, and saw the snow cannons firing along the slope. Each cannon had a beacon illuminating it, so the slope above Fontana Fredda was dotted with these fireworks, jets of water spray that froze upon contact with the air. He thought of Santorso leveling piles of artificial snow in the dark of night. He went back to the room with bread, cheese, and olive pâté, slipped under the covers, and Silvia pulled him to her immediately. Her feet were cold.

He said: Let's try again. Silvia at twenty-two.

At twenty-two I worked in a bookstore.

In Bologna?

No, in Trento. I have a friend from there, Lilli. After Bologna she went back home to open her own place. I've always liked books and by then I was done with college. When she asked me to come up I didn't give it a second thought.

So you worked as a bookseller.

Yeah, while it lasted. But it was a good time, you know? It was in Trento that I discovered the mountains. The Brenta Dolomites.

Fausto cut a slice of bread, spread the olive pâté on it, and added a piece of toma cheese. He wondered what it must have been like to discover the mountains. He brought the morsel toward her lips but stopped in midair.

So tell me, what are you doing under Monte Rosa?

I'm looking for a refuge.

You, too?

I'd like to work in a refuge on the glacier. For the summer, I mean. You know any?

Yeah, a few.

Can I have some of that cheese?

Fausto extended the slice of bread and toma, Silvia opened her mouth and bit into it. He inhaled her hair.

A refuge on the glacier, he said.

You think I can find one?

Why not? You can try.

Stop sniffing me.

You smell like January.

Silvia laughed. And what does January smell like?

What did January smell like? The smoke of a wood-stove. Dry, frozen meadows waiting for snow. The nude body of a girl after a long stretch of solitude. It smelled like a miracle.

3

The Cop

S antorso enjoyed not only the evenings when he drank, but also the mornings after. Not when he drank too much, so that he felt sick, but enough to carry the tail end of a bender into his waking hours. He would feel like getting up early and going out for a walk, and in those walks his senses were clouded in one way and sharpened in another, as if in the general opacity of the world, certain details became more vivid. The first was the water from the fountain: outside the house he washed his face and took a cold sip. Fontana Fredda, as the name would suggest, actually had several "cold fountains." At one time they were all troughs for livestock, water that flowed summer and winter at the same temperature, getting there from the glaciers by mysterious and underground routes. Both the water and the village sprang out of a wide terrace that ended abruptly, then dropped down five hundred meters to a wooded slope; uphill it rose more gently in a series of summer pastures. Now the pastures were silent and deserted, the dry stacks for manure empty, the bathtubs turned over in the meadows. Under the uniform gray sky, Santorso saw that a veil of snow had remained in the shaded areas, and nocturnal passersby had left their tracks on that veil. The paw prints of a hare among the fir trees, of a fox curious about the closed cowsheds. The hooves of a deer venturing out of the woods up to the paved road, attracted by the salt scattered over the frost. Still no sign of wolves. In the autumn they had been sighted just two valleys away, so he was sure they would come, or maybe they were already there but on their guard, studying the situation. Where the snow vanished, the stories stopped, like the things he only half knew. His father had a rule that he always tried to follow—never come back from the woods empty-handed—and that morning he picked some juniper berries, filled the little pocket of his hunting jacket with them.

It was Wednesday and there would be very few skiers on the slopes. He passed by the restaurant, but Babette hadn't arrived yet. There was only the cook, or rather that cook who wasn't a cook, working in the silence of the kitchen. When he heard the door, he went out to the bar and said hello.

Coffee? he asked.

You're Fausto, Santorso said. Actually no, you're Faus.

Faus?

Yeah, Faus, like false cook.

The cook laughed gladly. He filled the espresso compartment, turned the handle, and said: Sounds perfect.

Looks like it's gonna snow, Faus.

About time.

Babette came in with the sack of bread and the newspapers. She left the newspapers at the bar and took the bread into the kitchen. After her came the old dairy farmer who lived in one of the houses below. It was a beautiful time of the morning, between eight and nine, when the skiers had not yet arrived and the old people of Fontana Fredda stopped by Babette's, and there was talk of hay and milk, of wood supplies, of the snow in the past, when it piled up to the balconies. Fausto made coffee for himself, too, and Babette replaced him at the counter. Santorso glanced at her, raised his chin, a private code between them. She snorted, took the bottle of brandy, and poured a dash into the cup.

So, any wolves come? the farmer said.

Let 'em come, Santorso said. Everyone's welcome here.

I'm warning you, they touch just one of my animals and I'll go out there with my rifle.

Good.

You think I'm kidding.

No, no, I believe you.

And then what'll you do, arrest me?

Me? I am on leave, I don't arrest anyone anymore.

The girl, the new waitress, came down, too. She took an apron from under the counter and tied it around her waist. She poured herself a glass of water from the tap and drank it in one gulp, then she poured herself another. You're really thirsty, Santorso thought.

Fausto said: What do you mean, on leave?

I used to be in the Forestry Corps.

A forest ranger? But aren't you a hunter?

One doesn't exclude the other.

Imagine.

The girl filled a tray with glasses and went to set the tables. As she passed by, she touched Fausto's hand, and Santorso would have preferred not to notice. He didn't like the affairs of humans. He preferred those of wolves, foxes, and grouse.

I'll put on the polenta, Fausto said.

You're hunkered down pretty good, go for it.

You said it.

Au revoir.

Santorso finished his coffee, left a coin on the counter, and said goodbye to Babette, who was already doing something else. For the old farmer he didn't waste even a nod. Outside he took a breath and thought: Someone got laid here tonight. And then: What a beautiful smell when the snow comes. With the taste of coffee and brandy in his mouth, he lit a cigarette and at that point started thinking about what to do with his morning.

4

The Avalanches

Now it was really snowing. In a couple of days it would blanket the gardens, woodsheds, manure piles, and chicken coops. It was a thick, wet snow that didn't look like January snow, and it came with a wind that blew it sideways, encrusting the tree trunks and outdoor tables of Babette's Feast. Not many orders came in, and since there was a shovel next to the door of the restaurant, at three on Sunday afternoon it was Silvia who remembered to go out and start shoveling the small terrace.

She was struck by Fontana Fredda's transformation. The agricultural landscape she had found in December—countryside, only more rugged and wooded—had been transformed overnight into a boreal landscape. She looked at the road, where cars pulled out of their parking spots with clumsy maneuvers, fishtailing slightly. The stiff-footed people returning with skis on their backs. Not much snow fell where Silvia had grown up, and she wondered if her mother had ever seen what she was seeing, whether she would like it or not, feel protected or threatened. She watched the snowplow go by and clear the road up to the bend after the restaurant, forming a pile a couple of meters high. Then it turned around and Silvia understood how that barrier, in winter, became the border of civilization: she would be venturing into that white expanse beyond it at her own risk, and she got the urge to go see what it was like. That virgin snow attracted her more than the ski slope.

At the bar it was time for snacks, Babette's special chocolates. She reminded Silvia a little of her mother: a talent for serving and a total lack of interest in picking up dirty cups. Silvia went around the tables, dodging skiers and their children. She filled a tray and loaded the glass washer. After the washing cycle she put the cups to dry on the espresso machine.

What's it like outside? Babette asked, shaking a canister of whipped cream in vain.

It's not snowing anymore. They've cleared the road.

You like the snow?

I don't know yet. You?

Who ever sees it anymore? Snow brings work. Jesus, listen to me talking.

You finished the whipped cream?

Looks that way.

I'll get you a fresh one.

She went into the kitchen, where the steam condensed on the only window. The cook was grilling her crêpes, Fausto was at the dishwasher rinsing the lunch plates. He smiled at her, his forehead gleaming with sweat; immersed in vapor, amid piles of dirty dishes, he managed to maintain that noble aloofness of his, as if he'd just come down off the mountain and stopped in to give a hand.

Hot there, chef?

A sauna.

How about a beer?

Why not.

Silvia went to the bar with the whipped cream and came back with a cold beer. Fausto started the dishwasher, she handed him the mug, and he took a good sip. He still had foam on his mustache when the rumble of thunder came into the kitchen, clear over the din of the bar. Silvia was rattled.

What's that? A thunderstorm in January?

No, an avalanche.

Avalanches make that noise?

Sometimes. If it snows for two or three days, as soon as it gets a little warmer they start coming down.

So Silvia went out to the terrace again to try to see the avalanches. She looked at the mountains out front, the side facing north of Fontana Fredda. She heard that rumble and crush, but less than before, and noticed a puff of snow among the rocks. Then another on a bluff, like a waterfall. The snow was giving way a little everywhere, collapsing where it was too steep or had accumulated too much, and it came down following the shape of the mountain, its rises and slides, settling lower. After a minute of watching, she saw a real avalanche break off in a gully. First she noticed the lightning, then after a delay the thunder reached her, deep and long. You couldn't hear it without feeling uneasy. The mass of snow rolled down for a long time, swelling as it dragged whatever white it came into contact with, and after it stopped there was a dark stain on the mountainside, like a wall where the plaster had cracked off. Silvia pressed her arms to her chest and stood there watching that distant storm.

5

An Evening of Wind

That same evening Fausto invited her to his place. The apartment he had rented was a relic from the seventies or eighties, with its lace curtains and doilies, hearts carved into the backs of the chairs, and edelweiss embroidery. It reminded him of the ski lifts in the valley, built when it still snowed at low altitudes and now left to rust in the meadows. Yet he loved that hole-in-the-wall like you do places where you can start over, full of promise and free from disappointment. There was nothing of him in there but his boots at the threshold and a few books on a shelf, a little radio and his notebook on the table. Silvia noticed it as soon as she stepped in.

You write?

When I have time.

What do you write?

Fausto took the book he had published years earlier from the shelf. Stories about couples, mostly. Couples who got tired of each other, betrayed each other, broke up or stayed together, only to get hurt even more. The kinds of stories that once interested him, and now seemed to have been written by someone else. Silvia turned the little book in her hands.

You weren't a bookseller yet, were you?

Not yet.

Anyway, it wasn't out for long.

Why not?

Didn't sell. Then the publisher went bankrupt.

And you haven't written anything since?

Not books.

She pointed to the notebook. Can I?

If you manage to decipher it.

Fausto had done some experiments in the fall. He would go for a walk with the notebook in his backpack and stop after two or three hours, up high, where the altitude inspired him, and there, sitting on a stone under the sky, he tried to put into words what was around him. He knew immediately that he had everything to learn. He felt like a musician who had changed genre and perhaps even instrument. He didn't know if those pages would amount to anything, but he liked working on them, and anyway he was tired of writing about men, women, loves.

This scene, Silvia said. With the stream at night and the deer coming to drink. Did it really happen to you?

Yeah, I like to sleep outside from time to time.

Sleep outside, just like that?

I have a good sleeping bag. It's sort of a late-summer ritual. I say goodbye with a night outdoors.

It's a beautiful page.

You think?

Yeah, it's beautiful. There's mystery to it, don't touch it.

Silvia in that room. With his notebook in her hands.

Later they made love the way they were learning, a way that was becoming theirs. They listened to the wind that had kicked up outside again. When Fausto went to load the stove, he heard it blow through the chimney and saw the flame stir. He remembered he had a bottle of wine somewhere, so he took it together with two glasses and went back. Silvia was waiting for him, sitting up against the headboard. She had put her sweater back over her bare skin. While Fausto was pouring the wine, she wanted him to tell her about how he had become a writer.

You know who ruined my life? Jack London. Because I didn't feel like I had any stories of my own, it was just the idea that seemed so adventurous. Writing, drinking, making ends meet. Having writers' girls.

What are writers' girls like?

They're crazy.

He handed Silvia the glass and got into bed with her.

Ah, but at twenty it was nice to believe as much. Feeling like someone who was chasing his vocation.

Vocation?

I dropped out of college because I was convinced that they had nothing to teach me there. I read everything I could find on my own. I used to write at night, or on the subway, or at the bar, that's what vocation was.

I never had one.

No?

I've always chased people. And chance a bit, too. Maybe I chased other people's vocations.

But you came up here by yourself.

Yeah, up here I did.

You know what I did as soon as I got copies of that book?

What'd you do?

I went to the registry office to have my identity card changed. I said I'd lost it. And under the heading for profession I had them put *writer*. I'd brought the book as proof.

Silvia laughed. Fausto emptied his glass in the name of the old days. She said: But then you didn't become a writer.

Yes and no.

How's that?

I learned how to get by.

Interesting. How do you do that?

That's too sad a story for such a beautiful evening.

Then I think I already know it.

They drank and chatted while the bottle lasted. He liked staying awake and talking to her almost as much as making love. Even that tourist lodging managed to feel like a home, and that bed with its Christmas quilt like their bed: their nightstands, their glasses, the smell of their sex in the sheets.

Silvia was beginning to feel sleepy. She was lying on her side when she said: You know, I found a children's geography book there in the bookstore. It said that climbing a thousand meters in the Alps is equivalent to moving north for a thousand kilometers.

Really?

Yeah, as far as the climate goes. Flora, fauna, and so on. It said that the climate changes much more quickly in altitude than in latitude, so even a short difference in altitude counts like a long voyage.

Nice idea.

In fact, I thought: not that bad for traveling the world with no money. I took an atlas and started doing the math. I looked at Berlin, for example: a thousand kilometers. London: also a thousand. But it's not like you go a thousand meters high and find London and Berlin, that's not how it works. But you know what you'll find three thousand kilometers north of the Alps?

What?

The Arctic Circle.

It's three thousand kilometers?

That doesn't work out?

Well, actually, yeah. Here at three thousand meters you start getting the glaciers. And how far is the North Pole?

A little less than five thousand kilometers.

That's like the summit of Mont Blanc.

That's right. If you climb to the top of the Mont Blanc or Monte Rosa, you can almost get an idea.

Fausto laughed. Silvia yawned. He said: So where are we here in Fontana Fredda?

What's the altitude at Fontana Fredda?

One thousand eight hundred fifteen.

Let me think. We should be between Denmark and Norway. Almost in Oslo, I'd say.

Oslo?

Or maybe a bit farther up.

Come to think of it, when the world floods, all these valleys will turn into fjords.

The Fontana Fredda fjord.

A gust of wind slammed the shutters, interrupting the game. Fausto got up to go to the door and saw Gemma, his old neighbor, pushing a wheelbarrow in the alley between the houses. She wasn't walking very straight, the wind and the snow were giving her trouble.

I'm going out for a second, he said. He put on a shirt,

trousers, and shoes, with no socks or underwear, and went out. He had to raise his voice to be heard by the woman.

Gemma, hello!

Good evening.

What are you doing?

I'm going to get the hay.

She was going to get hay as if it were the most normal thing at that time of night, with the wind blowing the snow and knocking tools off the ledges. At the age of eighty, Gemma still kept a cow in the byre under the house—milked her and had her impregnated every year—after the others had been taken away one by one as she got older.

Wait up, so I can help, c'mon.

No need.

C'mon, I'll get a little workout in.

He took the wheelbarrow from her hands and pushed it to a sheet-metal shed. From the woods came the crack of branches snapping under the gusts of wind. He pulled two bales of hay down from the stack and walked back to Gemma's house, where he rolled the wheelbarrow under the eaves. He grabbed a bale and pushed the door of the little stall open. He was hit by that smell he could never get used to. He held his breath in the room lit by a dirty lightbulb, amid the manure that caked the walls and the black flypaper strips full of dead insects. The cow turned to look at him, tail tied high with twine. There were chicken feathers all around and a rabbit in a cage that was too small, in the old hay.

You need anything else, Gemma?

No, no. Thank you, thank you.

Good night, then.

Goodbye.

Outside he breathed deeply again, got that smell out of his nose, and went home. At the door he stamped his boots to knock the snow off the soles. He saw that Silvia had fallen asleep, the pillow under her cheek and one hand under her pillow, the same position in which she had just been talking to him. Her hair was strewn around her, lips purple with wine. There she was, his polar explorer. Fausto undressed and lay down in bed beside her. He wasn't sleepy so he began to think of the sea, the sea that would one day flood the valley until it touched the villages of wood and stone, the cottages that would become fishermen's huts, and the light there and the brackish air, while outside the north wind wouldn't stop harrowing the Fontana Fredda fjord.

6

The Felled Wood

It wasn't just branches he heard breaking that evening. Trees were felled. When Santorso suggested to Fausto that they go check the damage, he lent him a pair of skis with sealskins, which Fausto had never used. They put them on after the snowdrift at the end of the road. All that was left of the seal now was the name; they were strips of nylon stuck under the skis so they slid in the direction of the fur and were blocked against the grain. Santorso showed him how to hook into the bindings and use the heel piece, but he didn't waste a word on how to proceed.

He said: I haven't seen anyone skiing in jeans since the eighties.

That's all I had.

If by chance you get caught in an avalanche, when they find you, they'll take you for a relic.

Then Santorso took off. The snow was deep and untrodden, and he followed the line of the road for a while, as fluid as if he were ice-skating. Fausto tried to imitate his movements and keep up with him, but he felt even more awkward than with snowshoes. His stride was too short, and he tended to lift his feet instead of pushing them forward. Santorso adopted the didactic method of mountain men: he just went, that's all. He kept going until a fallen trunk blocked the way, so he gave up on the road and bent down to adjust his heel piece, then set off up the steep rise into the woods.

It was the larches that had succumbed to the wind. The firs, though heavier-laden with snow, had held up. Some of the Scotch pines had come down, ripped out with all their roots like saplings, but the larches were massacred. Many had snapped halfway up, two or three meters above the ground, and the woods were full of these stumps, with the trunks hanging sideways or lying in the snow, the bare branches stabbing into the ground. The mixture of snow and scattered needles, snow and broken branches, snow and turned earth gave those woods such a woeful aspect, as if they had been vandalized. After a few tortuous rounds Santorso had had enough; he unhooked his skis, planted them in the snow, and sat down on a fallen trunk.

Dio faus, he said, which meant false god, god who doesn't exist. He lit a cigarette as Fausto labored to join him.

You know how long it'll take to clear all this?

How long?

Years. The whole valley is like this.

At least there'll be lumber to use, no?

I doubt it, there isn't a straight tree in this wood. Eventually they'll have to pay someone to take it away.

Fausto didn't know what to say. Melancholy had taken possession of Santorso, as if he himself had been attacked and beaten up. He took a drag of his cigarette and said: That's how it is, Faus. Wolves and wind.

Poor woods.

You know, they never were much of anything.

No?

Our old men planted this, before that it was all pasture. But it hasn't grown very well. It's not like you put some trees down and they grow. Things just ain't that simple.

So how are they?

Santorso pulled off a little piece of bark from the trunk on which he was sitting. Outside it was gray and wrinkled, reddish inside. It had the color of a living thing.

He said: You know, as kids they taught us not to climb larches. The *brenga* breaks easily.

Brenga is larch?

Yeah.

So what can you climb?

Firs. The wood's elastic, won't break. Can't you see how they all held up? Only nobody plants firs, they're worthless.

Too bad.

Larch is hard, more profitable, but lets kids fall off its branches and breaks in the wind. *Dio faus.*

The mountain man is a real surprise, Fausto thought. After a while he said: Didn't you like being a forest ranger?

Working in the woods, yeah.

So?

Then they turned us into a police corps. I didn't like it anymore.

Santorso snuffed his cigarette in the snow. He peeled the skins off his skis with a quick rip, rolled them up, and slipped them inside his jacket. He said: Keep them someplace warm. If you ever have to use them again. The glue won't stick in the cold.

I think I'll be going down on foot. Where should I leave them for you?

Keep 'em, keep 'em. Get a little practice.

Santorso threw his skis to the ground and hooked the bindings as if they were old slippers. He locked the heel piece for the descent and picked up the poles. Then he took off, slaloming between all those felled trees, and despite the shambles it was a pleasure to watch him ski over the fresh snow.

7

Babette and the Airplanes

Then came the cold bright days that Babette once loved so much; rather than the heart of winter, she referred to it privately as the jewel of winter. Subzero in the early morning, frozen snow crackling under her soles, the ridges below became dazzling blades against a sky so dense and full, so clear, that from Fontana Fredda, with the naked eye, you could see the wings and fuselages and even the rows of portholes on planes bound for Paris. The planes would shimmer in the sun. Sometimes, as she watched them go by, Babette wondered if you could make out Fontana Fredda from up there. Maybe it was precisely the moment in the flight when the pilot indicated the Matterhorn or Mont Blanc to passengers, or maybe it was when some passenger glanced up from breakfast and halfway between two world capitals saw snowy valleys and thought: Oh, look, the Alps.

She used to just be happy where she was, she would never trade places with that distracted traveler. Now she wasn't so sure anymore. She pulled the sack of bread out of the pickup truck, collected the newspapers, counted the cars parked at the start of the chairlift. If they made it all the way to the garbage cans, she would more than break even. As far as Gemma's hay shed, she would fill the restaurant. She had to go see Gemma one of these days and bring her the leftover polenta for the chickens, and maybe a piece of cake and some mandarins. The sack was too heavy to lift so she just dragged it across the snow, then up the steps and across the terrace to the kitchen.

Together with Fausto she decided the menu of the day, as well as what they called the workers' menu, lunch for the snowcat and ski lift operators. Twelve set menus at the price of ten euros each: first course, second course, side dish, bread, and coffee. Fausto never got over the idea that they always ate the same thing. How about a side dish of zucchini? he proposed.

They leave the zucchini on the plate, and we throw it out.

What about risotto instead of pasta? Radicchio and leeks?

Forget about it.

It was always pasta, meat, potatoes, cheese; all you had to do was substitute the meat with an omelet and you'd get a swell of griping from the tables. This was the kind of thing Babette was tired of. The fact that whatever you came up with to bring change up there, it was met with indifference, if not hostility, until you just gave up trying. From growing flowers on the terrace to putting vegetables on the workers' menu to organizing a theatrical show—dream on.

The old dairy farmer was at his usual table, and said: So, did you see the wind?

Sure did.

Never heard of a wind that could take all the woods down.

At least the wind took something down.

How's that?

Nothing. Just kidding. Coffee?

She had lunch at eleven with Silvia. Fausto didn't eat lunch, he said otherwise he would lose the desire to cook, but he enjoyed preparing something original for the two of them. That day there was orecchiette with fresh tomatoes, goat ricotta, and mountain thyme. Where did he get the fresh tomatoes in February? At Fontana Fredda it was like tasting an exotic fruit.

While they ate, Silvia wanted to hear more details about Babette's legendary arrival in the valley, the summer of thirty-five years ago. That story thrilled her as if she were talking about the birth of punk rock, or the fall of the Berlin Wall.

But you know, Babette said, it's not like I was missing out on who knows what in Milan at that time. I was born late. The seventies were dead and gone and my friends were only thinking about going to the stadium or doing heroin.

The stadium?

Yeah. Shooting up on Saturdays, soccer at San Siro on Sundays, a few concerts every now and then. It was sad. So I thought: You know what I'm gonna do? I'm gonna head up to a mountain pasture this summer, milking cows and shoveling manure.

And you never went back.

In the end no. Who would've thought.

There must've been a man somewhere in the picture.

Of course.

What was he like?

I wouldn't say good-looking. But pretty wild. In the mountain pastures we had a mule, and he would take me for a ride as soon as we got an hour free, then we'd climb down to make love behind a rock. It was so cold.

And your parents?

Poor folks. Once a week I went down to call my mom and tell her I was fine. She would scream and threaten me, say, You're a minor, I'll get the police to pick you up.

I'd say that I didn't have any more coins for the phone and hang up.

And how did it end with the wild one?

The way it ends with mountain men.

How's that?

They've got a rage inside that comes out sooner or later. Most of the time it comes out with alcohol. If I can give you some advice, do what you want with them but don't marry them.

I wouldn't even think about it.

And at precisely noon the mountain men came in their ski lift operator uniforms. They were short on time and very hungry, so it wasn't a good idea to make them wait more than five minutes. Silvia brought bread and cheese while Fausto put the pasta in the boiling water and fried the cutlets. Babette watched them from time to time: forced to drink water, they would cut a piece of toma cheese and chew it with incomplete pleasure, as if the cheese tasted bland. She used to offer them wine a few years back, but the lift managers got stricter. The last one to enter was the man who worked up at the arrival station, at twenty-three hundred meters, in the sun and wind. Winter at high altitude marked his face, he had burned cheekbones and wrinkles around his eyes, and he threw open the restaurant door exclaiming: Ugh, palefaces!

Babette couldn't help but laugh. Nothing doing, there was something about them she was still fond of. Were there any sunburned Indian braves to be found in Paris? The chief went to sit with the others of his tribe, Silvia brought out the pasta, and then the skiers started coming in with their boots, helmets, ski suits, and hungry children, and Babette settled behind the cash register to ring up receipts.

8

Hair

One evening Fausto's mood changed because of a phone call. He had been in the kitchen for a long time and Silvia had no intention of asking him who he'd been talking to or about what. She didn't want to know anything about his previous woman.

She said: If you're not into it, we can also do something else.

Sorry.

You shouldn't always say sorry.

Do I always say sorry? I must have made it a habit.

Outside it was snowing again, but in the apartment the stove was on and it felt good to be naked under the covers. She stroked his leg with her instep. She took his hand, her favorite part of him. A splinter of wood had lodged in his palm, and she gave him a kiss right there.

Maybe I'm just tired of winter, he said.

Isn't it a little early to be tired of winter?

It's March, I want to see the grass again. I want to go fishing, I want to swim in a stream.

You know how to fish?

No.

You want to take a bath together?

There's not enough hot water for a bath.

And to wash my hair? You want to wash my hair for me with these beautiful hands?

Fausto wasn't the type to refuse such a proposal. He got up and put on his pants. He loaded the stove, filled a pot of water, and set it on the heat. He brought a chair into the bathroom, spread a towel over the back, and made Silvia sit there, asking her to lean her head back over the tub. He was very professional. Then he wet her hair: it was full and thick and the shampoo made a lot of suds.

She said: Do you know that I may have found a refuge?

Really? Which one?

It's called Quintino Sella.

Quintino Sella on Monte Rosa?

I imagine that's it. Babette's a friend of the manager, I spoke to him this morning.

I know the Sella.

You do?

Fausto plunged his fingers into the suds, lathered,

thought, lathered some more, then said: Capanna Quintino Sella at the Felik, three thousand, five hundred and
eighty-five meters. I must have been eight or nine the first
time.

What's the Felik?

It's the name of a glacier.

They took you up there at eight?

Yeah, it was normal. There were other children. In the
beginning only up to the refuge, up and down in a day.
Once we were a little older, we would sleep there to go up
Castor the next morning.

Castor?

One of the Rosa peaks. Four thousand, two hundred
and twenty-six meters. One of the most beautiful.

You still remember the altitudes?

Who could ever forget them? Names, altitudes, you
know how kids are. Fausto took the showerhead and
started to rinse. He stopped when he felt the hot water
turn tepid. The electric water heater couldn't handle
Silvia's hair. Then he rubbed in the conditioner she had
given him.

Would I make a good hairdresser?

Excellent. Tell me about Castor.

There's a ridge to get there. From the Felik Pass, or
Felikjoch. In some places it's a real blade of snow, goes
straight down left and right, with these huge crevasses
opening at the bottom. As a kid they teach you that if the

guy in front of you on the rope line falls on one side of the ridge, you have to jump straight to the other, otherwise he'll pull you down with him.

Did that ever happen to you?

Just for fun. One time the guide reassured us and tried to get us to do it. One kid down on one side, and me on the other.

Yikes.

It was a blast.

Fausto went into the kitchen and came back with the pot of hot water. He said: Now keep your head back.

Like this?

Yeah. Close your eyes.

He poured the water directly from the pot, slowly, holding it by the handles.

Ah, Silvia said, that's wonderful.

Done. The polar explorer has a clean head of hair.

Thanks, chef.

I ain't no chef no more. I'm a *coiffeur*.

Alors, merci, mon coiffeur.

Then they went to sit in the kitchen near the stove. Fausto put some more wood in and she began drying her hair with her usual method. She opened the stove door and, one lock at a time, brought her hair close to the fire, combing it with the fingers of one hand on the palm of the other. She held it there for a only few seconds, so it wouldn't burn. Her hair was steaming.

Felik, Fausto said, was the name of a city in ancient times. One day a foreigner arrived. He knocked on all the doors but no one wanted to take him in, so as he left he cast a curse on them. He said: On this shitty town it will snow tomorrow, the day after tomorrow, and the day after, until it's buried under the snow. So now instead of the city of Felik there's a glacier.

Serves them right. Has it been a long time since you went back?

Must be about twenty-five years.

And if they take me, will you come up and see me?

You bet. Wait, let me show you something.

Fausto went to look for the 1:25,000 map and spread it out on the floor. The Capanna Quintino Sella was at the top of the map, at the base of the great Rosa glaciers. Each glacier had a name: Verra, Felik, Lys. The refuge was indicated with two black squares.

Why are there two?

The other one is the old lodge. They left it there next to the new one.

How old?

Must be from the nineteenth century. Or maybe it had already been rebuilt, I don't know. All those shelters have burned down a thousand times, lightning sets them on fire, avalanches bury them. I remember a bivouac blown away by the wind because someone forgot and left the door open. They came back in the spring and the bivouac was gone.

Really?

Those were the stories my dad would tell me.

He was a mountain climber?

Yeah, a weekend climber.

Fausto laughed. Talking about glaciers and shelters, he'd forgotten about his phone call. He looked at the map and noticed that, at the bottom, on the opposite side from the Quintino Sella, there was also Fontana Fredda. If the map was a meter long, they were about twenty kilometers as the crow flies. An idea came to him that he would need to look into, and he showed Silvia the trail to the refuge. The fire flickered through her black hair, and on the map the glacier was pale blue and white, marked with tiny blue veins.

9

A Cat and Two Blackcocks

Santorso's winter ended on a Saturday in March, at dusk. After lunch he slept like he rarely had and woke up tired, a little sore. At five o'clock he went to the garage and filled the snowcat up with diesel fuel while the last of the skiers, the stragglers who loved the late afternoon runs, were still coming down, drawing curves in the slush. At the end of the season the snow was already giving way at noon, later it would turn to mush; it looked to him like it was begging to go back to water, to be able to wet the earth and flow downstream. He saw the chairlift stop with empty chairs. He climbed into the snowcat's cabin and was grateful for the heating, the padded seat, the vibrating motor massaging his back. After the last skier, the patrol passed by to close up, collect poles and signs, make sure there was no one left, and in the meantime he heard his colleague following him on the radio; he pushed the two levers controlling the treads forward and set off. Below him the slope was riddled with dark spots. In the season's last few weeks his work would be reduced to patching and mending, removing snow from one side to cover a hole on the other, making it through Easter and then letting that blessed snow do what it pleased.

And yet he liked that job, he could be alone in the mountains and watch the night come. He would drive his snowcat through the long shadows of the larch trees in the low sun. He didn't run into anyone, except Fausto, who was climbing the edge of the slope with his skins. The ski patrol must have turned a blind eye to him: after all, he was the one who put pasta on his plate every single day. You could see he must have been training since the last time, starting to make some headway, although in jeans and a plaid shirt he looked more like a woodsman than a skier. The two snowcats passed him and he waved to them with his pole.

Who's that? the other snowcat driver asked over the radio.

Babette's cook.

Well, wha'd'ya know.

Then he and his colleague separated where the track forked. Now that he no longer had anyone in his mirror, he lit a cigarette and turned on the music. He passed the chairlift station and continued along the beaten path the cats used to maneuver and stopped near a large boulder that emerged from the snow. The snow was still high and compact up there. It was the snow he would use for the holes at the bottom of the slope. But for now he took out his binoculars, opened the cabin door, and sat on the treads, scanning the edge of the woods.

He knew where to look and that evening he finally found them. Two fully grown blackcocks against the white snow, in the thick of combat. Black grouse always chose the same places to fight; from one year to the next they returned to their arenas. They came out in the last light, with the sun already gone over the crests but not yet extinguished, the hour the French called *entre chien et loup.* Santorso liked that way of saying it. Between dog and wolf, between twilight and darkness, the blackcocks came out to scrap, they used their claws, beaks, wings, everything they had to fight—so fiercely at the beginning of the mating season that they would ignore a caterpillar-tracked bulldozer, a man with binoculars, and even rock 'n' roll. Santorso could see the two blackcocks' beautiful red eyebrows, feathers fluffed to frighten their opponent. Somewhere even the grayhens were waiting for the winner. Snow or no snow, for him that had always been the start of spring.

10

The Gas Pump

For the animals, love was beginning, and for the two of them it was ending, or suspended. On Easter Monday the chairlift stopped one last time, the skiers left Fontana Fredda like migratory birds, and Babette prepared a CLOSED FOR VACATION sign. She announced that she was going to an island whose name or sea she did not want to divulge. She paid everyone's wages, added a small bonus, said nothing about how the season had been, but on the last day a guy in a suit and tie appeared and sat down with her at a table, going over bills. Fausto knew enough about debt for that scene to spark his desire to rebel.

He went out with Silvia the following Thursday. They went down to Tre Villaggi, where some places were still open. They had never gone out for dinner and felt a little uncomfortable as a couple in a pizzeria. Without their cook and waitress aprons, without their bed and stove, without their pillows and glasses, they were, again, a man of forty and a girl of twenty-seven, whose paths were about to separate.

So where are you going for spring?

To Trentino for now. There's a lot of work in the countryside this time of year. You know, vegetables and orchards.

You don't want to hang around here for a while? You can stay with me.

I've already half committed with my friends. But don't worry, I'll be back!

Sure.

And there's Quintino Sella this summer.

I know.

And you?

I have to take care of some stuff in Milan. Then, who knows, I might go pick some vegetables myself.

He hadn't thought of getting her a gift, whereas she had. It was an edition of Hokusai's *Thirty-six Views of Mount Fuji*. Fausto knew little about either Japan or the history of art, and he knew only the most famous of those drawings, without ever having really looked at it. Now he found out it was called *The Great Wave off Kanagawa*. On closer inspection, he realized that the gigantic wave was overwhelming three small fishing boats, and that under its seething crest, in the center of the drawing, you could see a small snow-covered volcano, Mount Fuji. The contrast between the impassivity of the mountain and the tumult of the wave in the foreground was evident.

He leafed through other pages: Tell me about this book.

It's from 1833, Silvia said. In Japan it immediately became a great success, these were the prints people would hang in their houses. They're all views of Fuji, but the real subject is the daily life in the foreground. Work and the passing seasons. At least I think so.

They look very modern.

They do. They struck a lot of the Impressionists.

What was this Hokusai guy like?

Someone who made thousands of these drawings. He was like a manga artist, a hard worker. He signed them, The Old Man Mad About Art.

The Old Man Mad About Art!

Each view had a title with the name of the place and the description of the scene. They were all farmers, fishermen, carpenters, busy at work and almost always unaware of the mountain that guarded them, sometimes huge above their heads and sometimes tiny on the horizon. In one view, some elegant women are pointing to Fuji from the terrace of a tearoom. And in another, toward the end of the book, there's only the mountain, a full page.

But the cook and waitress aren't there, Fausto said.

No?

And neither are the lovers.

Well, we know they're there.

It's a beautiful gift. Thank you.

It was their last evening, so instead of going back to Fontana Fredda, they decided to keep it going in the valley's bars. The tourist bars were all empty and melancholy, but they found one, under the roof of a gas pump, where the locals celebrated the end of the ski season. Off with their company uniforms, their last wages in their pockets, and no blood alcohol tests for the next six months. Everyone was having so much fun that Silvia began dancing among the tables, and then Fausto saw what she meant when she told him she was good at partying. She swayed her shiny, black hair back and forth, the men whistled, everyone in the room's attention was focused entirely on her. Two beers came that she hadn't ordered and he looked for whoever had offered them. A guy with a crazy smile raised his glass at him from the counter.

She came back to the table and he said: That's it, the party's over.

Why?

Because now each person has to buy a round for all the others. Your fault. I'm saying goodbye before I pass out.

Silvia took a sip of beer, grabbed his face with her hands, and gave him a kiss. She was sweaty, turned on by the dance and the looks, and already a little drunk.

She said: But we're not over, right?

Aren't we?

No, we're not.

I thought it was just a winter thing, he said.

What do you mean?

To stay warm in the winter.

She knitted her brows, then tugged at his beard to punish him for that bad joke. She said: You're not gonna turn bad on me being up here all alone, are you?

I'm not alone. Look at all these people.

Come on.

I won't. I promise.

You want to leave?

Dance one more, I really like it.

The music drifted out of the small bar and someone was smoking outside, someone else stopped for gas. Those who stopped saw the party and went in for a drink. The woods rose past the houses, black and indistinct to the height of the meadows, where the snow reflected the moonlight.

11

An Empty House

When he finally decided to do it, one morning in April, Fausto got into his car early, before the sun poked up over the Finestra Pass. A few stretches of pasture were now emerging from the snow, but it was old, grayish grass, and it seemed to smudge the white like the stove ash thrown out of the houses and the piles of manure that were starting to smell again. A little farther down they would set that grass on fire, and it would leave blackened strips of burned pasture. After a whole winter at high altitude, Fausto felt a sort of amazement as he descended into the valley: already at Tre Villaggi the snow had almost disappeared, and the grass was taking on color below a thousand meters. The fir and larch woods filled with birch, oak, beech, maple, and chestnut trees became denser and more luxuriant, and the stone of the

51

houses was replaced by bricks and tiles, and finally by concrete depots. At the tollbooth it was natural for him to turn on the radio, and he hit the eight o'clock news. It all converged: the valley floor, the highway, the trucks, eight in the morning, the day's negligible news. He'd been out of it for a while, but it wasn't like the world had ceased to interest him. He stopped at the highway rest area just for the pleasure of drinking a coffee among the truck drivers and commuters. On the Turin–Milan highway, Monte Rosa stayed in the window for kilometers, first over the fields and farmhouses, then over the shopping centers and warehouses on the outskirts. Mount Fuji above the factories and morning traffic, he thought. It wasn't even nine thirty when he got to Milan. He had always liked the absurd proximity of the Alps to his city. How many times had he left for the mountains at the last minute, on an impulse, after an argument, or because he wanted to be alone? He just had to jump in the car and he'd be up there in a couple of hours. Now he would have preferred the two halves of his life to be more distant, the journey to be long and complicated, a story of trains, carriages, mule tracks, like in the diaries of nineteenth-century English travelers.

In line at the traffic lights he thought: God, you really get used to everything. I might even get used to this again, it would take me a week. It was automatic for him to take the ring road, turn after the Ghisolfa Bridge, find parking in the usual side street. Peruvian delivery boys coming and going in the neighborhood square, idle Egyptians sitting at outdoor tables, tall thin Senegalese waiting for the laundry outside the laundromats. Humanity was like the forest, he thought: the farther down you went, the more variety there was. He entered a courtyard surrounded by little yellow buildings, the recycling bins on one side and the bike rack on the other, and used his keys to open a door that had a bench and some flowers in front of it. He had prepared himself for a sad sight, but when he crossed the threshold it was his sense of smell that was struck: not the smell of abandonment but the unmistakable, mysterious smell of home, still so present. Yet there was hardly anything left of the furniture, except for the kitchen that wasn't worth dismantling and a sofa they had wanted to get rid of for years. A few posters on the walls, a few bare shelves. The apartment had a high ceiling and large windows; in a previous life it had been the workshop of a craftsman, and Fausto climbed an iron ladder to the loft he'd inherited from those times. Upstairs, Veronica had left him a roll of black bags and a stack of cartons. She hadn't touched his clothes in the closet or his books on the shelves. His things and hers, separated neatly, without resentment, in what had been their bedroom. Fausto appreciated such care, he saw in it the desire for a dignified conclusion.

He packed a load of stuff to throw away, went to the

landfill, went back to a bar to get two cold beers. Veronica arrived as he was closing the boxes of books. In the house there was no longer any table or chair, or cup or glass or ashtray, so she drank her beer leaning on the kitchen counter, flicking the ashes from her cigarette into the sink, and he sat on the old broken sofa. They had greeted each other with a kiss on the cheek. Only one, not two, detached but not formal. When he used to come back from the mountains, the first thing Veronica would do was undress him and send him under the shower. When he kissed her, Fausto remembered that, and he was ashamed of the smell he must have had on him. He should have showered first.

She said: How'd it go up there? Are you writing?

Not so much.

What did you do all winter?

I cooked.

Cooked?

In a little restaurant. A nice place, you know? Better than many other jobs. Simple menu, always the same four dishes.

Who would've thought.

Not me, that's for sure.

Well, you always did like to cook.

That's true.

You're not taking your equipment, your nice pots?

I wouldn't know where to put them. You want them?

Me, cooking? Veronica smiled. Maybe it's time I learned. That way I'll stop ordering junk food every night.

She took a sip from the bottle, showing her long neck. After more than six months apart, Fausto saw her as a beautiful woman of forty, in the season when women in Milan are starting to undress. Their bare skin was something that always struck him, in the spring, coming down from an altitude where women were still covered in wool. Their arms, ankles, calves, and the shapes that could be sensed under the fabrics. Veronica's was a more mature and fuller body than the other one he had recently become accustomed to. But she had definitely lost weight. So much for junk food. He wondered if it was because she didn't feel like eating or because she was going out with someone.

Are you doing well? he asked.

She shrugged her shoulders. I have a job and they pay me. Considering the times, that's already something.

And apart from work?

What should I tell you? This is not where I imagined being at this point in my life.

I'm sorry.

But it's not like you helped much.

You're right.

Did you know your mother calls me once a week?

No, I didn't.

But you remember she's eighty, don't you?

I'll go see her tomorrow.

Do you ever think of others while you go about your happy degrowth?

That was Veronica. Everything she said was true and right, no denying. So Fausto went on apologizing to that beautiful woman for whom he had cooked so many, many times.

12

In Another Country

He saw her again the next morning, in an office in the center of Milan, halfway between the Duomo and Piazza degli Affari, one of those marble-clad buildings full of nothing but lawyers, accountants, and notaries. He sat down at an oval table with Veronica, the notary, the man from the bank, the young woman who was going to live in their house, and her father, who was buying it for her. Because of the economic crisis they were selling it for a little less than they had paid, and most of the money went to pay off the mortgage that had been, for the two of them, the equivalent of a marriage. The bank representative had the look of someone who had to slog through many notarial documents. The young woman was eager to have the keys, her father was the only one following word for word, Veronica just wanted to get it over with, and Fausto felt as if he were listening to their divorce ceremony: *Do you, Fausto Dalmasso, wish to renounce this woman, no longer share your life with her, take back half of what you had together, and never again make love with her, no longer take care of her, free her from the encumbrance of your person, and have nothing more to do with her until death makes ground meat of you both?* Yes, I do, he thought, and he signed where he was supposed to sign. He wished the young woman happiness in her new home, that it could be an important place for her, and that she could spend her best years there. After the signatures, the father distributed the envelopes with the cashier's checks, one to the bank, one to Veronica, and one to Fausto, who slipped a little more than eight thousand euros into his jacket pocket. At the age of forty it was all he owned, except for the car, and he stepped out of that office part bitter, part lighter.

So goodbye, he said to Veronica on the street.

How sad, eh? she said. Her eyes were moist. What are you doing, going back up right away?

I'm in no hurry. You want to get a coffee?

No, I have to go to the office. I'm late already. And to say what? Bye, Fausto, take care.

A kiss on the mouth this time. Then she turned and walked quickly down the avenue. He, who was in no hurry, watched her back until she disappeared under a portico, into a crowd.

When will I ever get back to the center of Milan, he thought, so he decided to take a walk before leaving again. He almost didn't remember the Duomo, the large piazza with its paving stones freshly washed, the equestrian monument to Vittorio Emanuele, the austere palazzi of the nineteenth and twentieth centuries that balanced the cathedral's Gothic oddities. He remembered Hemingway and that story about Milan he had read so many times, what was it called? "In Another Country," that's it. There was the canal that still passed through the center, an old woman selling roasted chestnuts on a small bridge, an American veteran who bought some on his way to the hospital and kept the warm chestnuts in his pockets. It had to be October or November. There were foxes and deer hanging outside the shops, their fur ruffled by the wind, their bodies swaying, and after therapy in the hospital the soldiers would cross the square to go to the Caffè Cova, near La Scala theater, full of patriotic girls. Fausto remembered the opening words: "In the fall the war was always there, but we did not go to it any more." What a memorable opening. He would have liked to read it to Silvia in their little room. He was practiced at reciting it out loud, because he had used it for years in writing classes, and when he explained it to students he talked about taking care to heal, healing and sharing one's wounds with others, the impossibility of recovering completely, and yet the possibility of finding consolation. Now he preferred to remember it as a story about Milan in 1918. A time when game was sold in the shops throughout the center. He wouldn't talk to Silvia about wounds and healing, if anything about deserting: at the front the war is always there, but let someone else do it, we'll go around with roasted chestnuts in our pockets and buy the girls drinks at the bar. Thinking about it made him thirsty. He crossed the Galleria, happy he could still find his way through the streets of Milan by heart, and reached the Cova, which was no longer next to La Scala but in Via Monte Napoleone, among boutiques frequented by the wives of Russian millionaires. Or were they lovers? He ordered a goblet of champagne at the counter to toast his recent fortunes. He had just divorced and sold his house, he thought, and he was drinking champagne alone at ten in the morning. The barman must have been used to the strangeness of the Russians, and he served it without flinching.

13

A Hospital in the Valley

When Fausto returned to the shop where he would buy groceries, he heard that Santorso had been in an accident. They didn't know exactly what had happened to him, except that he had been in the mountains and had to be taken away by helicopter, but in the village there was a rumor that an avalanche had caught him. Fausto tried to find out at the newsstand and then at the bar. Everywhere he went, they'd heard about it, but they didn't know, they didn't understand why this guy was getting involved, this cook who had been staying up there out of season. Maybe because of the things that had just happened to him in the city, Fausto decided to really get involved. He didn't need to ask where to go, the helicopter came and went from one place only.

He drove fifty kilometers to a modern provincial hospital, well signposted and with a large parking lot, at the foot of the mountains. Already in the car it occurred to him that he didn't even know Santorso's name. But he had some experience with hospitals, he'd been to a few. He asked about an uncle who must have come from the ER, he was probably in Orthopedics, and he used one of the two surnames that almost everyone in Fontana Fredda had. He hit the bull's eye on the first shot. There was a Luigi Erasmo Balma laid up on the third floor.

He found Santorso, or Luigi Erasmo, in bed with a bandage on his head. He had two more around his hands: two swollen bandages like boxing gloves that reached to mid-forearm. He was awake; more than awake, he was on edge.

He said: Well, look who's here.

Luigi!

What brings you here?

What brings me? I was looking for you.

You were looking for *me*?

What did you do?

They had to get over the awkwardness. Santorso adjusted himself with his back against the pillow and Fausto glanced at his roommate: an old man with a middle-aged woman sitting next to him. The woman was looking at them, too, then to avoid being intrusive she turned and went back to deal with her father, or whoever he was.

Stupid move, Santorso said. I lost a ski, and instead of leaving it where it was I thought I'd go down and get it. It was a bit steep, I went down some rocks and set off a slide.

Where was this?

You know the Valnera?

Of course I do.

You know the ridge with the avalanche fence?

Yeah.

Back there, in no special place. I was looking for grouse.

And you fell?

No, I held on. But maybe I would've been better off falling.

He tried to raise his bandaged arms, looked at the ceiling of the room, and said: As soon as I heard it rip I held tight against the rock. I more or less protected my head, but my hands took it full-on.

Fuck.

It was like putting them under a tractor wheel. At least I had my heavy gloves.

They're broken?

I don't know in how many places anymore.

And your head?

Yeah, well, never did use it much.

He still had the fear in his eyes. He was weak and out of breath from talking about it. It was impressive to see him under the sheets, with his stringy hair, unkempt beard, neck dark from the sun, and those clean white bandages. Still, once he got over the surprise, he seemed glad to have a visitor. Talking and telling his story gave him back some spirit.

You came a ways to find me.

I wasn't sure I should come, then I thought . . . Thing is, no one up there could tell me anything.

Up there! They had me left for dead.

More or less.

I look like I took a beating.

In fact, you did.

A nice blast of wind, eh, Faus? You remember that day in the woods?

Yeah, but it didn't knock you down. You're a real *brenga*. Did they do any surgery on your hands?

They need to wait until the swelling goes down a bit.

Right.

They talked for a few more minutes, then a nurse came in with the medications and Fausto thought it was time to say goodbye. He asked Santorso if he needed anything and promised he would be back in a few days. Santorso wasn't used to this kind of attention; he forgot to thank him but was moved when he said goodbye. He entrusted himself to the nurse's care with the same embarrassed gratitude.

Fausto went to look for a doctor and found one almost immediately. He was a man of about sixty, with a tanned face from life in the open air, accustomed to speaking simply. He told Fausto that he'd seen hands that mangled before, in factory workers who got them caught in the hydraulic presses. It wasn't clear how Santorso had managed to use them to call for help; he must have done so immediately after the accident and before they became unusable. He'd lost a lot of blood, passed out in the helicopter from bleeding, and was now full of antibiotics and blood thinners. Still, even though the doctor ruled out that those hands could go back to how they were before, they would somehow get them working again.

He wanted to add something that had nothing to do with orthopedics: he told Fausto that Mr. Balma's general condition could be defined as disastrous. He had an alcoholic's liver and his hardened arteries were clogged, he could expect an ischemia at any moment, if not worse. He hadn't seen a doctor or had a blood test in years. Typical mountain man.

He started speaking in the plural, saying *them* instead of *him*, and said: You yourself know what they're like. With what they eat, they get to their fifties with more fat than blood in their veins. And it's not like they change their habits. They seem to be waiting for the inevitable.

Fausto nodded, he didn't know what to say.

He's not your uncle, is he?

No.

Doesn't that man have any relatives?

I don't know, I'll have to ask.

Well, if you find anyone, tell them to come and see how he is. In three days you're the first person I've spoken to. And then someone will have to help him when we send him home; with two hands in a cast he won't be able to do much.

I guess not.

Leaving the hospital, more out of curiosity than anything else, he went to see the mountain rescue helicopter. It had taken him an hour to drive from Fontana Fredda, but as the crow flies it wasn't that far, it must have taken five minutes. He found the crew there near the helipad. He recognized the guide, he was famous in those parts. His name was Dufour, he'd had a career as a mountain climber and belonged to a historical family of Monte Rosa guides; they were the managers of the Quintino Sella refuge. Even though he was close to retirement age, he still took shifts on the helicopter. Dufour also seemed to recognize him. For a moment Fausto indulged the illusion that twenty-five years later the man would remember that little boy on a trip with his father. Instead he heard him ask: Aren't you Babette's cook?

In the flesh.

Then I know who you came here for.

Not that he minded being Babette's cook. It's only right that your job should be what gets your face remembered among the thousands of faces passing by and getting confused with one another. Not traipsing around the same mountains since childhood or feeling homesick when you were far away from them.

Dufour said that he was the one Santorso had spoken to on the phone. The two of them had known each other for a lifetime. He had given him his position in detail, the altitude, the visibility, the description of the place where he was. He wasn't hard to spot in the snow. He was sitting on a rock as if he were enjoying the view, and when the helicopter came he raised his arms in the agreed signal. Those hands were an ugly sight.

Fausto told him what the doctor had said, not about the heart and liver, but about the hands. The factory workers' hands caught in the presses, hands that would somehow work again.

Thank God, Dufour said.

He'll need to be patient.

I should think so.

Can I ask you something else?

Sure.

There was a girl who worked at Babette's this winter. I know you might be taking her on at the refuge.

Yeah, we are.

I'm glad.

You think she'll make it? She's not gonna bail on us after a week, is she?

No, no, she won't bail.

What's her name?

Silvia.

That's right, Silvia. And yours?

Me, Fausto.

Come and see us sometime, Fausto.

Gladly.

He could have talked for a long time with a man like Dufour. About the Sella, about Monte Rosa, about the glaciers of the past and all the mountains he must have seen in his travels around the world, but he thanked him and said goodbye to the helicopter pilot and went back up to look for some relative for that poor devil.

14

The Outlaw

And so the thief stole down into Fontana Fredda as soon as the guard wasn't there. He had come from the east, from the Finestra Pass, before first light. He was a lone wolf who wandered from one valley to another, staying in the woods and crossing the roads only when necessary, and only at night. At that hour the snow was still frozen and held him up well, so he reached the pass leaving no trace but for the scratch of his nails on the steep part. He went past the small chapel, the dry stone wall that had once been a boundary, and looked out onto the small plateau in that predawn gray.

Sniffing the air, he sensed a distant memory of those places, a memory received as inheritance. Like the rules he obeyed without reservation—stay high, stay in the woods, travel at night, stay away from houses and roads—even though he now realized that something had changed since the days when the rules had been established. Someone in town must have already been awake. He smelled the fire, which was the smell of man, and the smell of his cattle, but they were far fainter than when he, or someone before him, had been chased out of there.

The wind changed direction, caressed the mountain, and brought him the scent of the woods. He smelled chamois, deer, wild boar: much more game than there once was, when his forebearers had to lie in wait whole days to find a dormouse or badger, food that didn't fill and forced them to always be hunting. Now his adversary had gone away, left the field free. In the woods, prey abounded and hunting became easy. The wolf raised his snout to the wind, waited for it to turn again and bring him more news from there, and then the confirmation: the scent of man was now the tail end of a scent, the trace of someone who has passed by and is no longer there. He looked at the uncultivated fields, the extinguished chimneys, and it seemed to him another of the uninhabited villages he had encountered on his journey. Yes, his adversary had lost vigor, maybe not to the extent that he had become harmless, but enough so he could risk it. Maybe the old rules needed to be changed.

He also felt something else, which had nothing to do with hunger, hunting, fear, prudence, calculation. It was what he felt every time he reached a ridge and looked out over a new valley. A kind of excitement, a smell that attracted him even more than that of deer or chamois. The smell of discovery.

The chapel had seen thieves, poachers, smugglers, and outlaws of all kinds pass by. The wolf came down the hill, silent and light on the hard snow in the open field, until he found shelter again in the thick of the woods.

15

The Mountain Man's Daughter

It turned out that Santorso did have a relative, a daughter who lived somewhere else, whom he hadn't called. Eventually she found out what had happened. She also rang Fausto, shortly after hearing from her father. Hard to tell from her voice how old she was. She asked for more precise information about him; Fausto told her about his visit to the hospital and repeated to her what the doctor had told him, without omitting anything this time. The girl asked further questions: Would her father report a disability? Was he able to work or not? Was he entitled to a pension? She saw the matter from a very practical perspective. She spoke the language with almost no accent: only certain closed vowels betrayed the Fontana Fredda lingering in her, little defects she hadn't been able to get rid of, and which to a trained ear revealed the hard mountain tongue.

Are you a friend of my father's?

I'd say so.

I know you met each other this winter.

That's right. I was the cook at a restaurant on the slopes.

My mother's.

What?

My mother's restaurant.

Babette's your mother?

Yeah, but that's not really her name.

It immediately seemed so obvious to him. Santorso passed by there morning and evening, she treated him as if he were her brother. Fausto felt stupid for having seen them together for months, and not realizing it.

The girl said: You don't know my father very well.

Actually, no.

But those who do know him didn't go see how he was doing.

Fausto didn't know what to say. He felt like he'd just gotten cornered by a child.

Well, thanks anyway. I appreciate it. Now I'll look for a flight for tomorrow.

A flight from where?

London.

You live there?

In Brighton. It's on the sea.

And what do you do in Brighton, school?

No, I work in a hotel.

Is someone picking you up at the airport?

Yes, don't worry.

After hanging up, Fausto spent the whole evening thinking about it. He thought about Santorso and Babette as husband and wife. Who knew how long they'd been together and how long since they'd broken up? The daughter could have been twenty. With such a father and such a mother, it's logical that she had a certain character. The daughter of a revolutionary woman and a mountain man.

He'd never had a child with Veronica. They'd talked about it a few times, postponing the discussion for the future, and then there was no longer any future. And now who knows if it was better or worse, not having had a child together? Some remnant of their relationship, maybe far away, in a hotel by the sea. Someone who looked a little like her and a little like him. He thought of calling Silvia to tell her about what was new, but going into such things wasn't a good idea, so he let it go. He felt very lonely that evening. What was it she'd said to him? Don't turn bad on me? He thought of Veronica's back as she hurried away so he wouldn't see her cry. But what was he doing there, a forty-year-old fool with no family and no job, if not chasing the ridiculous utopia of *living-in-the-place-that-makes-you-happy*? There was only one person he could turn bad on, and he knew how to do it, too. He poured the rest of his glass down the drain and headed for bed, straining to keep his promise.

16

Songlines

What can I eat, then? Santorso asked.
    Peas. Beans. Chickpeas. Soy.
Disgusting.
You know, it depends on how you cook them.
And meat?
Chicken.
Chicken isn't meat.
It's white meat. And fish. Smoked salmon, filet of cod.
And cheese?
You can forget about cheese.
Dio faus.
They were returning from the hospital. Fausto was
driving, Santorso looking out the window on a rainy
morning. At first he was brooding but when they entered
the valley he paid attention to everything. He had spent

three weeks in there and told the nurses that he hadn't been away from home so long since his military days. In three weeks, spring had transformed the landscape: the grass had grown a span, the fruit trees had blossomed, the deciduous forest had taken on a brilliant tone. In the mountains the snow line had risen five hundred meters.

My valley's beautiful, isn't she? Santorso said. He didn't even notice the rain beating on the windshield.

Beautiful she is.

And some people are running away.

Go figure.

Easy here, this is where they take them up.

Fausto slowed down behind a herd of cows occupying the road. They were going up to the *mayen*, the May pastures, the intermediate ones. For a kilometer he stood in line behind the long procession of cattle, indifferent to the rain, the cowbells around their necks, the dogs barking around them and occasionally shaking the water off their fur.

What did you go to Milan for?

I sold an apartment. I went to see my mother. I took back my books.

Why, you had an apartment?

Split in two, with my ex. Now we have nothing, split in two.

Well done.

I guess. I don't know.

And now what'll you do, buy a house in Fontana Fredda?

No. No more houses. For now I'm looking for work. Babette might be on vacation, but I still have rent to pay.

That's right.

Then the cattle left the paved road and spilled into a meadow. A big man with an umbrella and a farmer's apron exchanged a greeting with Santorso as they passed by. Santorso raised a plastered hand and said his name. Good-looking Martín, he said. He named everything they came across, every house, village, person, every stream and every pasture, but in a low voice, his own private litany. There goes Cold Hollow, Slab Meadow, the Overhang, there's Crooked Man and Lost Bread Creek, and look at Time-to-Kill at the Trois Villages bar . . . Fausto was reminded of that book by Chatwin about the Australian aborigines, who memorize their trails with songs instead of maps. In the song there was everything encountered along the way, a strange-shaped rock, a lonely tree, someone's field, and so the traveler, learning it by heart, also learned the trail. Santorso was singing his way home, his valley songline. Fausto wondered if sooner or later he would be singing it, too.

And what did they tell you about drinking?

They didn't say anything to you?

Not to me.

You can drink a glass of red wine with meals. And a beer from time to time.

That's already something.

I'm wondering how you'll manage without hands.

I'll figure out a system.

At Tre Villaggi they turned toward Fontana Fredda, and from there, as they went up little by little, May faded and died out. At fifteen hundred meters the larches still hadn't put out their leaves, the first crocuses sprouted in the pastures, and only the torrents were surging. After the last bend, now at eighteen hundred, the rain turned to snow.

Siberia, Santorso said. It was the last verse of his songline.

And they say it's spring.

Fausto drove him to the front door of the house, where his daughter was waiting for him. She was a tall, sturdy young woman, with her father's somewhat hardened features and the very fair complexion of redheads, like her mother. The red that lingered in Babette's hair as a memory still burned in hers, it was the red of poppies and stood out in that gray landscape. She opened the car door for her father, who struggled a little to get out with those two arms hanging from his neck. They entered the house while Fausto unloaded the boxes of peas, beans, tofu balls, and frozen fish he had gotten for him.

17

A Postcard

But you couldn't stop spring. The instinct to melt, open, and sprout was too strong. Fontana Fredda's fountains gushed into their overflowing troughs and the torrents of meltwater dug out ruts in the dirt roads and uncovered the stones on the paths. The sun warmed the walls of the terraces, waking the vipers from their hibernation. Fausto would occasionally see them mate, down in the place they called the Murazze: the vipers, usually so shy, lost all caution and it became dangerous to cross their paths, you'd find them twisted together and it was better to give them a wide berth. He resumed walking for hours as he did in the fall. He would climb up to the snow line or wander through the wounded woods, where red and roe deer rubbed their heads against the trunks, bleeding, scraping the velvet to finally free the new rack of antlers.

In those days he went back to leafing through the book that Silvia had given him, their secret Hokusai. There were a thousand correspondences between those ancient prints and what he saw from the window. In Fontana Fredda, the locals burned junipers and brushwood, pulled the harrow to level the molehills, Gemma went out with a small knife to collect chicory: alone in the middle of a pasture, she bent down every two or three steps and filled whole bags. There, too, everyone seemed to ignore Fuji watching them.

At the end of the book he found the only writing that Hokusai had left, which said: "From the age of six I had a mania for drawing the shapes of things. When I was fifty I had published a universe of drawings. But all I have done before the age of seventy is not worth bothering with. At seventy-three I have learned something of the pattern of nature, of animals, of plants, of trees, birds, fish, and insects. When I am eighty you will see real progress. At ninety I will have cut my way deeply into the mystery of life itself. At one hundred, I will be a marvelous artist. At one hundred and ten, everything I create—a dot, a line— will come alive. I call on those who may still be alive to see if I keep my word. Signed: The Old Man Mad About Art."

Babette was still missing from Fontana Fredda; the sign outside her door kept fading. Fausto felt like doing something he hadn't done for a very long time: he took a pad and a pen and sat down at the table to write her a letter. He remembered how much he used to enjoy it; that was his first form of writing. How many letters had he sent to the girls he'd fallen in love with! In three pages he told Babette about that spring, about Veronica and about the house in Milan, about the doubts and the sense of failure that his days in the city had left in him. Then about Luigi's accident and meeting her daughter, who looked so much like her. He wrote to her that, despite her griping about it, she seemed to have accomplished something good in Fontana Fredda: namely, a very fine daughter, and a place that for many was a refuge, in the truest sense of the term. It certainly had been for him, who found acceptance and understanding at a complicated time in his life, esteem for his limited culinary virtues, and cheer when it was twenty degrees below zero outside. He reminded her that, in Blixen's story, during the famous lunch that had cost Babette a fortune, not one of the Norwegian bumpkins had any idea of what delicacies were passing under their noses, apart from the retired general who had lived in Paris for years. In silence, since he could not communicate it to anyone, that old soldier ate and thought: This woman is a great artist. Come to think of it, that was what made all the difference in the story: one of them had seen her, recognized her, and Babette's feast was worthwhile if at least one person in the world enjoyed it.

Finally he wrote: And how are you? We miss you. Are you coming back?

Then he went down to Tre Villaggi, to the newsstand, and asked for a postcard from Fontana Fredda. The newsagent fished out a packet from the stock. There was one with a vintage photo: Fontana Fredda in 1933, only a handful of stone houses, no road, no light poles, no tourist villas, no Babette's Feast, and no chairlift; only a farmer pushing an ox up a mule track, and the mountains. Beyond the cultivated fields and the haystacks, the mountains were timeless. Fausto folded the letter into the envelope with the postcard and wrote the only address he had on the back, that of the restaurant—with the hope that, wherever she was, Babette would have had her mail forwarded. Though really, what would change if she read it in a week or a year? He was glad he'd written those things to her. He stuck a stamp on it, posted it just outside the newsstand, and it seemed to him that it was leaving on a very long journey.

18

Old Wood

Santorso's house, whitewashed and facing south in the full sun, was a little higher up from the village. It was a farmhouse, or at least it had been conceived as such, and though the hayloft was still in use, the stall had become a storeroom, crowded with tools and memorabilia and spoils from his walks in the woods.

This here is the cave of wonders, Fausto said.

Or the landfill.

It used to be a cow stall?

In theory. My father built the house, but he hated animals and always worked as a stonemason. Maybe he was hoping I would go back to the tradition, and as you can see . . .

No cows.

What can you do? There's hunting dogs and there's sheepdogs. Everyone follows whatever instinct they got.

And what'll you do with the hay?

Sell it, trade it. I like old wood.

There was a stack of grayed planks on one side, against the wall. Many of them were still encrusted with manure, the kind of manure that looks like it's been there for centuries amid the mountain ruins. Some planks were warped from the dampness, others full of bent nails.

All larch. Seeing them like this they're crap, but look how they turn out when you clean them up.

He couldn't show it with his hands, so he pointed with his foot: a board he had washed and brushed until the grain of the wood stood out and the gray had veered toward a bright red.

But is this its natural color?

A little is the red of the larch. A little is all the shit it's absorbed. You can't even get the smell out anymore.

And what are you going to do with it?

I was thinking of a table. Now I won't be doing anything anymore, it'll have stay here and age a bit longer.

Fausto sniffed that wood: it had a strong smell, but not unpleasant. It was spotted with the holes of nails that had been driven in. Each hole had a darker red halo, rust from the nail.

Santorso sat down against his carpenter's bench. He

cleared his throat and said: I may have found something for you.

Something?

A job.

With wood?

No, with logging sites. Down in the forestry department they've made up their minds to clean up the woods, and they're putting teams together. I still know someone there.

Logger teams?

Yeah.

And where do I fit in? I've never picked up a chain saw in my life.

I thought you could cook.

Fausto put down the plank and turned his attention to him.

The teams, Santorso said, are made up of ten or twelve loggers, plus a cook working half a day. The sites are too far away to come down for lunch, better to have someone cook up there on site. You go up in the morning with the groceries, you have a camping stove, pots, all your stuff, and by two o'clock the shift is over. They usually take a girl, but I said to myself . . .

That would be great for me.

If I wasn't hurt, I'd go up myself. They pay well, you know. And it's for the whole summer.

The whole summer in the woods.

Cooking, you know how to cook.

By now, I'd say so.

So I'll give them a call.

Cooking at a logging site: Fontana Fredda was already giving Fausto Dalmasso, the writer, a couple of lessons. One: you always need someone to cook; whereas someone to write, not always. Two: it was true, Santorso was a man who never said thank you and probably never said sorry, but he knew how to repay a debt, and this itself was worth more than words.

They went into the house, where his daughter had made tea. They sat down and Fausto immediately noticed the stuffed grouse, it was perched on a branch sticking out of a board mounted on the wall. It had a blue neck that stood out against the black plumage, its wings outspread in a battle pose.

Is that a capercaillie?

A black grouse. The capercaillie is a mountain grouse, but it's been extinct here for a while.

I'm going out, his daughter said. I'll take the car.

Bye, baby, have fun.

Bye, Dad. She bent down to kiss her father on the cheek. Don't get yourself too tired, now.

Yes, ma'am.

Bye, Fausto.

Bye, Caterina.

She was stern, that girl, stern and suspicious, but at least she'd begun to call him by his name. Santorso let a minute pass, then pointed to the cabinet behind Fausto and to a bottle without a label. It was transparent, you'd think it was grappa. Fausto thought that for once they could even make a toast. He dumped the tea, poured the liquor into the cups, and pushed one forward.

You have kids? Santorso asked.

Me, no.

Think about it. I'm fifty-four. It's nice to have some youth around.

I'll think about it.

And your girlfriend, how's she doing?

My girlfriend? Ah, no. She's not my girlfriend.

Too bad. She was cute.

Santorso was all proud of how he was hooking Fausto up and wanted to chat. He pinched the cup with his two casts, managed to bring it to his lips, and took a sip. You could see it was a well-tested technique.

He said: This is gin, I make it myself.

You make gin? How do you do that, with a still?

No need for a still. I take vodka, which tastes like nothing, and put juniper berries in it. Try.

Fausto tasted the liquor and was surprised: it was gin, impossible to detect the trick. It was a good gin that wouldn't have been out of place in any of Milan's down-town bars.

I like it because it tastes like the woods, Santorso said, then he emptied his cup to the health of his cook friend, that false cook who for some reason had taken a liking to him.

19

An Outpost of Humanity

She was cute, yes, and in early June she was in a jeep going up the southwestern slopes of Monte Rosa. Dufour's son was driving, and next to him sat a man named Pasang Sherpa. Nepalese, Silvia thought; she had already heard of the Nepalese who worked at the Rosa refuges. She had slept badly, and her dreams extended into her waking state, making her melancholy. Yet she was leaving for her great adventure: in half an hour of dirt road they went from the woods where it was already summer to pastures not yet in bloom, passing ski slopes and the pylons of closed cable cars, up to the first patches of snow. This here is France, she thought, this is Belgium and Holland, here is Denmark, Sweden, Norway. Did her mother also appear in her dream? She felt the same way she did whenever she dreamed of her. In

Norway the snowfields were furrowed with tire marks. Dufour's son had to shift into the low range gears and managed to keep going for a few hairpin turns, but then had to give up, well below the pass where the road, in theory, ended.

End of the line, he said. They went out into the early morning air and unloaded the rucksacks, crampons, and rope, and put on the down jackets from the jeep. It was too overcast to see Monte Rosa and they were at the altitude where the clouds turn to fog, and vice versa.

From the window Dufour's son said: You have everything, Doko?

I think so.

Then to her: Pasang knows the way. When you get tired he'll carry you on his shoulders.

Let's hope not.

Well, have a nice walk. *Tashi delek.*

He turned the vehicle around and disappeared down toward the valley, and soon the sound of the engine was lost in the wind. Pasang chose a pair of crampons and bent over at Silvia's feet; he adjusted the size, hooked them on, and strapped them tight as she offered him first one foot and then the other, ashamed of not knowing how to do it on her own.

We're not on ice yet, are we?

No. But with crampons it's better.

What did he call you? Doko?

That's a joke between us. It's a kind of basket.

Like what porters carry?

Yes.

Is that why your name is Sherpa?

Pasang shook his head and smiled. He must have explained it many times but he still had the patience to repeat it. He said: Sherpa is the name of a people. We all call ourselves that.

How ignorant of me, sorry.

It's the people who live around Everest. Many of them work as porters, that's why you get confused.

And what does Pasang mean?

Friday.

Friday?

It's because I was born on a Friday. He laughed. He had large white teeth and a smile that narrowed his eyes. I'm just a Sherpa born on a Friday.

You speak excellent Italian.

No, that's not true. And what does your name mean?

It means woman of the woods.

Silvia, woman of the woods?

More or less.

Beautiful name.

Then the Sherpa tied the rope to his rucksack, carried it over his shoulder, and set off in the direction of the pass. The snow was frozen and Silvia immediately appreciated how useful the crampons were. She followed him silently, adjusting to his tracks and pace. She had understood that this climb was a test for her. Otherwise why not take them up in a helicopter, along with all the rest? But it was right that way, you had to earn a place at the refuge. More than a thousand meters of altitude difference had to be taken calmly, without looking up too much or thinking about how much farther. She decided to focus on Pasang's feet in front of her. Her feet, the snow, the regular cadence of her steps, and she felt her legs gradually come out of their torpor, her heart and lungs found their rhythm. She'd been training over the spring. The fog around her stopped seeming hostile to her, there were only her feet and her breath to think about, only her, Pasang, and the snow. Under all the layers of winter clothing, her body began to heat up and sweat.

Then in her concentration the dream resurfaced: her mother was telling her not to go up there to the refuge, because they needed her at home, and Silvia was arguing about it. She said: So all those stories about raising kids with freedom and courage are only good for others and not me? Her mother answered: Look, it often takes more courage to stay than to leave, and with those words she always won, it made Silvia so mad. In the dream her mother was still a young woman, she could have been forty-five, and Silvia felt like a girl.

She didn't even notice that they were at the pass until they reached the cable car terminus. It was a disturbance, a violent interference: the ugly structures of machinery, safety nets, dugouts, rough concrete. Pasang passed by without stopping, turned north along the ridge, and shortly thereafter the trail markers disappeared under the snow. Silvia felt disoriented: partly because of the wind blowing up there, partly because of the altitude—she had climbed too quickly. Only the night before she was on a train crossing the cities and fields of summer. Now the wind opened glimpses through the clouds, she raised her eyes up from Pasang's feet, and in those gaps she sometimes found the blue of the sky, sometimes a quick vision of rocks, ice, peaks. Peaks she didn't recognize. In the snow a row of footprints, chamois or ibex maybe, veered off in a different direction from theirs, and she found herself thinking: If I were alone, I would be lost. Between the snow and the fog I could wander up here until nightfall, and then it would be the end of me.

Pasang saw that she was lagging behind, or maybe she had already decided where to take a break, so he placed his rucksack under a rock that sheltered it from the wind. They had been walking for nearly two hours.

We're going good, he said.

What altitude are we?

Three thousand meters. Hopefully more.

So this is the Arctic Circle, then. The fog allowed for a peek at the two valleys at their feet: the glacial moraines, the white torrents, the first meager pasture grass, everything was now beneath them.

I've never been so high up.

Never?

What's three thousand meters like in Nepal?

It's countryside. You have rice paddies.

You grow rice at three thousand meters?

Yes, and barley higher up.

Pasang unscrewed the lid of the thermos and filled it with tea. He offered it to Silvia instead of drinking it himself, and she again wondered if he was doing it out of duty, because they had entrusted her to him, or just out of kindness.

The tea was good, hot and strong, very sweet. That man, his pace, his speech, his tea, had the power to soothe her.

And have you ever been on Everest?

A few times.

A few times at the summit of Everest?

At the summit only twice. Other times below the summit. There's a lot of different jobs for an expedition.

For example?

Do you want to come and work in Nepal?

I wish!

There are those who bring material to the base camp. It's hard work, but not dangerous. Then those who prepare the glacier with fixed ropes and ladders. This is dangerous because of avalanches. Then the high-altitude porters, very dangerous. And there's even the cook.

There's always a cook, isn't there.

For me it's the best job. It's safe, you stay warm, you get to eat well. But the one who goes to the top of Everest is the best paid, and he makes a career.

He makes a career and comes to Monte Rosa to work?

Hopefully, yes!

Silvia had dry fruit and chocolate in her rucksack. Pasang accepted the chocolate readily; he broke off a nice big piece and that made him happy. They drank another sip of tea and set off again before they cooled down too much.

From there onward it was all rocks from which the wind had swept the snow away. Below, there was a series of small basins, little icy ponds not much more than puddles. Then the ridge got thinner, its slopes steeper, and it became a rocky crest. They began to find fixed ropes and steel ladders, she had to use her hands, and Silvia was happy because this kept her from getting distracted, lost in her thoughts, and feeling guilty because she was disappointing her mother. She knew the rocks better than the snow.

Not much more to go, Pasang said.

It's fun.

Do you climb?

I've climbed a bit.

So we'll go this way?

Sure.

She followed him for a stretch of almost vertical steps and ropes. A wooden bridge placed right on the crest to span a gap between the rocks. A sharpened passage, flat sheets pitched to make them seem like a slide into the void. Maybe she was lucky to have that fog hiding the precipices from sight, it presented one problem at a time and the problem was immediately before her eyes and under her hands, but right there Pasang saw something he didn't like.

Maybe I should tie you, he said.

Here? Aren't we almost there?

Yes, but it doesn't look good. It'll take two minutes.

Silvia didn't want to argue, but she felt diminished. The crest wasn't that special, in the Dolomites she had been on much worse, she would have liked him to go on and trust her. She wanted to at least tie the knots herself: she put on the harness, tightened it, took the working end of her rope and tied herself with a double figure-eight loop, then she waited for Pasang to get over the passage, fix a lanyard around a rock spike, and secure it.

Come on. Plant the crampons well.

Not until she was on the pitched sheets did she notice the veil of ice covering them. Pasang was right, it was a treacherous spot. Her crampons had to find purchase on a few millimeters of ice, which she crossed quickly and decisively, grateful for being tied. He repeated the process at one other point, a channel full of hard snow where he had to dig out steps with his ice ax, and for the rest of the way they went without protection until the end of the crest. Lucky for her they had arrived, because the thirty-five hundred meters were going to her head: she felt confused, emptied, she watched her feet and hands move almost without having to command them.

The Quintino Sella refuge finally appeared on a plateau at the edge of the glacier. It wouldn't have looked out of place as an Arctic base: a large building shaped like a trapezoid fallen on its side, with solar panels covering one of its faces. The old wooden refuge was a little farther, a real pioneer cabin, with the latrine shed protruding out onto the cliff. In front of the new refuge, on the plateau, little Tibetan prayer flags were fluttering. They were strung from a tall stack of stones to smaller piles scattered around. The colored flags put a little cheer into that damp and foggy morning.

On the helipad Dufour was sorting the contents from their big sacks. They were full of supplies, cases of beer and wine, packs of toilet paper and other stuff that had to be taken inside. There was already work to do.

Oh, Doko, the guide said. How nice to see you.

Hi, boss. We made it.

20

The Loggers

In the woods, though, there were no exotic Nepalese, there were men from Bergamo and Valtellina, and Moldovans who spoke Italian with a Bergamo or Valtellina accent. Fausto climbed toward the site among hundreds of trees marked red by the forestry department because they were broken, crooked, sick, or at risk of falling, and he listened to the woodsmen shout. Even the chain saws had a language: after a month he had learned to recognize the voice of a Stihl, a Husqvarna, the cut on one side of the trunk and the main cut on the other. One of the saws had a drier sound, as if someone had gotten the fuel mix wrong. A cut was interrupted by the blows of a mallet against the wedge slipped in so the trunk wouldn't bite the blade. Then came the cry: *Timber!* and Fausto stopped. He heard the crackle of the fracture, a sinister noise that made you look for shelter, and finally the thud of the fall. A thud muffled by June's already thick foliage. Now he saw where the tree had fallen, not far from him; between the branches of those left standing a piece of the sky that hadn't been there before opened, and the sun lit up the undergrowth.

He reached the shipping container that served as a kitchen and removed the fresh bread and groceries from his rucksack. In the middle of four blackened stones he piled larch sprigs picked up along the path. He took a sheet of newspaper, crumpled it and set it on fire, then slipped it under the twigs and stayed there blowing until the flame kindled to life. When that beard of moss growing on the trees was dry, it caught fire better than paper. For Fausto the smell of burning larch was the best: a scent of childhood summers that always brought him back home.

The chef has arrived, one worker said, sniffing the air.

Ciao, chef! another shouted from a distance.

The loggers had the same tastes as the chairlift workers, always pasta, meat, and potatoes. Still, Fausto liked to change things up with his variations and make himself liked. That day he made potatoes alla Mario, a recipe taken from a story by Mario Rigoni Stern: he boiled them in the copper pot until they almost fell apart, then he fried up four chopped onions in a lake of butter and threw the potatoes in. He let the steaks go on the stove with rosemary. The pot was used again to cook two kilos of spaghetti; he threw them in at a quarter to noon. There was also a call for lunch that the guys from Bergamo, who were sticklers for punctuality, taught him. *It's hard!* he shouted at noon, meaning the polenta was firm, though that day there was spaghetti alla carbonara, then he drained the pasta and threw it into the frying pancetta. The chain saws fell silent one after the other, it was as if they could smell the aroma.

They would have lunch in that makeshift trailer even if the sun was out. Those who worked outdoors for eight hours didn't mind eating indoors with their legs under a table. That day Santorso also passed by. His casts had recently been removed. Except for the scars left by the surgeon, his hands looked like normal hands until he had to use them, and then you could see how little he could do. Among the loggers he found comprehension. While Fausto served the steaks and potatoes, he heard them discuss work accidents. They told stories about trees freaking out and falling on the wrong side, or turning like tops as they fell, or bouncing off the ground in unpredictable ways, cracking heads and breaking backs. And then of distracted loggers who had split open a forehead or leg by being too casual, and in fact, after lunch, they didn't cut trees anymore. Fausto served coffee and put the bottle of sambuca on the table, so whoever wanted to could spike theirs. Santorso poured himself a whole cup with a labored movement, and then, as the others got up with toothpicks in their mouths, listlessly stepping back into motion, he came out to sit in front of the languishing fire.

He wasn't used to watching others work. The loggers started piling up branches, trimming trunks to be dragged away with the tractor. Fausto burned the paper plates and napkins, poured the last hot water into the pots with a little detergent, pulled up his sleeves, and started scouring.

Santorso picked up a handful of sawdust and wood chips scattered all around. He brought that poor hand under his nose and said: There's a chain saw here that's lost its edge.

Oh yeah?

You can see it from the shavings, the finer they are, the blunter the blade.

I get it.

You know what this smell is, Faus?

For Fausto it was the smell of resin, of fresh wood, an intoxicating scent that spread out from the larch stumps and stacks of logs and that carpet of shavings that covered the ground. In the evening he removed it by getting undressed, then put it back on in the morning with his shirt from the day before. But he wanted to hear it from Santorso, so he said: No, what smell is it?

It's the smell of clear-cutting.

Good, isn't it?

Damn good. You know how long it's been since I smelled it? Must be forty years.

That was when I was born.

Who knows if I'll ever smell it again.

Cut it out, you're in better shape than me.

On the roads they passed the herders heading up to the mountain pastures, and one of them stopped with a tractor and trailer. He asked if he could load up some branches for a bonfire. Then Fausto remembered that it was June 29, the Feast of Saints Peter and Paul. In other valleys they built bonfires on the Feast of Saint John, but they were still fires meant to celebrate the solstice, and they'd been making them long before those saints existed.

I wouldn't know, I have to ask.

Sure you can, Santorso said. Take all you want. It's just gonna sit there and rot, you'll be doing them a favor.

The herder loaded the whole trailer bed, then left with it all filled up and wobbling toward his cow stall.

21

Bonfires

It was after ten that evening when the tail end of that long June sunset finally burned out. Then all over the mountain pastures the piles of timber, heaps of branches, boxes, pallets, feed bags, and old tires were sprinkled with gasoline and set on fire. Santorso saw them light up one by one, a little higher than two thousand meters; on the dark slopes of the mountains the bonfires shone and competed with one another to be the highest and brightest. He counted five, six, seven. They faded out and lit back up with a gust of wind. Not even someone like him could be indifferent to that vision. The fires announced that there was still someone up there in the mountains, that that life existed, in case people down below had forgotten.

He went for walks in the evenings, that way he'd be

cutting into his drinking time. His hands hardly worked, but it's not as if his legs were much better after months of infirmity. He was forced to go up slowly, choosing the easiest trails, listening closely to any warning his heart might be giving. Riding up from the hospital with Fausto, he felt the altitude for the first time in his life: his heart in his throat and the shortness of breath, even though he would never admit it to anyone. The only person he could talk to about it had left Fontana Fredda without even leaving him an address.

The sky was dark now, even that last hint of summer twilight had gone. All that was left of the distant bonfires were embers. The stars, however, gave off some light, and he never liked using a flashlight, which was more for others to see you than for you to see the world. Whereas the eyes sharpened to capture new reflections and outlines if given the time to adapt. What he saw that evening was the carcass of a chamois on the banks of a stream. It was at a point where several rock slides converged in the winter, there were still traces of them on the slopes, and at the first of them Santorso thought of one of those animals getting surprised and overwhelmed, buried under the snow till it reemerged in the spring and became a meal for the foxes and crows. He approached to get a better look and judged from the horns that it was a good ten years old, which was old for a hunting area. Then he realized that it had been gutted, but freshly, and the innards were still there, a few meters away from its body. That chamois might have been killed that same day. His hunter had picked out the intestines, which disgusted him, then moved them away to eat the heart, liver, and lungs. The meal was interrupted, disturbed perhaps by someone's arrival, and that someone may have been him. Santorso looked around. In the darkness he saw nothing but rocks and the reflections of the stream.

So now you're here, he thought. Welcome. I guess there are those who leave and those who come back, no? Those who croak, those who fuck, and those who go hunting. The world belongs to whoever takes it.

Within a day the whole chamois would disappear, so he thought of taking something, too. Maybe those beautiful black hooks. Once it would have been enough to get a good grip on them, twist, and pull hard: the horn's hollow sheath would have detached from its bone base, there was nothing but tissue to hold it. Now his hand was barely able to get its fingers around the hook. With his left hand he held the animal's head and with his right he tried to pull, but he felt his fingers slip away.

22

The Night Owl

That night Silvia's alarm clock rang at three. She wasn't really sleeping and turned it off before it disturbed Dufour's daughter, with whom she shared the room. She took the headlamp and toothbrush from her bedside table, put her pants and jacket on, then went out. It was traumatic to go from the heat of the duvet to the cold of thirty-five hundred meters, a few degrees below freezing, the wind that never stopped blowing at that altitude. In the bathroom she was welcomed by the strong smell of latrine, ammonia and industrial deodorant. But at least the wind died down in there, it only made the panels vibrate, although she still felt it coming up from the squat toilet when she pulled down her pants. The drain was nothing but a pipe on the glacier, and the cold coming through forced her to do everything in a hurry.

She brushed her teeth with freezing water, washed her face and ears, took her headlamp and pointed it to check herself out in the mirror. Look at those dark circles under your eyes, she thought. Do you know what time it is? In a month her face seemed to have aged ten years, from the altitude, the erratic sleep, the wind and fierce sun.

When she came out of the bathroom the glacier was luminescent. It gathered the glow of the starry sky and sent it back into the night. In front of that sight, when she was alone, Silvia felt she was in the presence of a celestial body, a planet perpetually burnished by wind. No other sound came from there, it was a desert—still and perfect and white. As she turned toward the valley she saw the lights of the villages two thousand meters below. There it was, the old blue planet. She felt a sharp pang of homesickness for it. She was close enough to make out the streetlamps, the odd cars along its roads, the gas stations. She thought that down there, just a little while ago, kids were drinking beers in the square, smoking and chatting, with music coming out of the clubs. On the old blue planet, on that big mess of a planet, summer had just begun. Then she felt cold again and went back inside.

In the kitchen she put the big pot on the fire, sat down to warm herself by the stove, and was able to take off her windbreaker. She ate a few biscuits in the time it took the water to boil. She had procured Fausto's book, down on the plain, and read a story about a man and a woman at someone else's wedding who decide to break up. She found it good if somewhat mannered, the imitation of writers he had obviously been reading at the time. Here and there she could hear a voice that was trying to emerge: clear observations, little truths about love, and she imagined a bolder Fausto than now, less ironic and doubtful. In the story there were beers, highways, rest stops, cigarettes, and no mountains. It was strange to think of an age in Fausto's life when the mountains weren't there.

At around four she threw a whole box of tea bags into the pot, added half a kilo of sugar, and began funneling the tea into the thermoses with the ladle. Someone started the generator and the lights came on in the kitchen. Then Pasang entered, sleepy and cold.

Were you working in the dark?

Yeah, it's quieter.

Is there any tea?

Sure. With lots of sugar, just like you like it.

Never enough sugar.

You're right.

Upstairs the alarm clocks started ringing, the floorboards creaked. The first to get up were those leaving to traverse the Lyskamm peaks, the sleepless faces of those who had been tossing and turning for hours. Only the guides were able to sleep before the *Man-eater*. They had breakfast, exchanged a few words in German, Polish, and Flemish, then put the thermoses in their rucksacks. In the entrance hall they wrapped themselves up for the ascent, then went out onto the terrace to put on their crampons and harnesses. They set off on the glacier in ropes of two or three, rows of little lamps that drifted away in the dark.

At that point they were all getting up. The mountaineers crossing the Lyskamm Nose, then those headed for Castor, and finally the few going nowhere, who would have kept on sleeping if not for the bustle. Dufour's daughter also came down. Her name was Arianna. She was thirty years old and had spent summers up there since she was a young girl; the refuge for her was sort of a family restaurant. But she had also studied, traveled to India and Nepal, and in the winter she was a yoga teacher. With Silvia she was immediately protective.

How's the headache?

A little better.

I'll have a coffee and then give you a hand.

Take your time.

Have you been to the bathroom? What's the situation?

Pretty nasty, rough night.

When Arianna took over, Silvia was able to go out and get some air. It was clear outside now, but the eastern peaks of Monte Rosa hid the sunrise and the whole glacier was still in the shade, bluish like the sky. Only at the top, at about four thousand meters, did the dawn suddenly light it up; she saw the first ropes up there, at the Felik Pass, in the sun. On the terrace, pitted by generations of crampons, high mountain sparrows perched together with the black choughs, the last living creatures on the edge of the glacier. With a frightened air, feathers puffed up from the cold, they pecked at the crumbs on the floorboards—pushed up to that height by who knows what instinct.

Pasang came out of the latrines with the bucket and rag. Just another one of the tasks they all took turns with, but Silvia was thankful every time it wasn't hers. Whereas he always seemed to be in a good mood.

Pasang, can I ask you something?

Of course you can.

You who've been there plenty of times, have you understood why they go? What is it up there?

Wind.

Wind?

And snow.

And then?

Hopefully sun. If not, then there's clouds!

The Sherpa laughed. Twice atop Everest, but it was impossible to wring any philosophy out of him. When talking to him, everything in the world seemed to simply be: bucket, rag, wind, sun, snow.

It was seven o'clock when the last climbers finally cleared out. Now there was time to rest a little, and Ari-

anna called her over to have breakfast. She'd turned on
the radio and set a small table for two: a cup of coffee
with milk, a piece of cake, a little music, that gentle girl,
and even the Arctic base managed to feel cozy, almost
home.

Eighty-nine this morning, Arianna said. They eat, shit,
and leave.

Right.

Tell me the truth, it's not what you expected.

No, but I'm happy to be here.

Swear?

I swear. Kind of proud of myself, if I must say. You
know, once in a while I think: If my mother could see me.

What's your mother like?

What *was* she like. She's not with us.

Oh, sorry.

No, go figure. She was a cheerful woman. Died two
years ago.

Was she sick?

For a while.

What did she do before that?

She was a teacher. Italian, in middle school. The kids
in the neighborhood all remember her. Even some who
went places, fortunately.

And you?

I was jealous. I'd cause trouble to get myself noticed
by her.

Who knows why she was now launching into that story, with a girl she barely knew, at seven in the morning in a refuge on Monte Rosa. The effect of the altitude, probably. Outside, the light changed color as the first rope lines reached the top slopes of the four-thousanders.

23

A Marsh

Then the sun came out from behind the Punta Parrot and Vincent Pyramid; for the long summer hours it beat down on the glacier, and the layer of snow covering it thinned day by day, revealing crevasses and seracs and bands of grayish ice, which by afternoon were veiled with water. Now it was nothing more than an old glacier in retreat, but in its heyday it was well advanced. It evoked fear, rather than today's pity: mountain passes abandoned because no longer passable, valleys relegated to legend as lost paradises. As for those who ventured there, no one knows the number of deaths it still stored. They say it takes seventy years for the glacier to return those it has taken; when they disappeared they were young and strong, they fell along the way to some peak, and when their children were old, a ragged boot, a wooden ice ax, or some other museum piece would peer out from down below, where they had been dragged. Monte Rosa was dotted with crosses and plaques in memory of these dead, with names, dates, even photos. Every summer a priest would go up and say mass at that high-altitude cemetery, he would bless the shelters, their keepers, and the climbers going up, and remember with a prayer those who had never come down.

One day in July, Fausto also found his sanctuary. At three thousand meters he happened on a hollow where the first meltwater torrents crossed and formed a marsh, between granite humps smoothed out by the retreating glacier higher up, beyond a rocky strip traversed by thin cascades. In that hollow, some erratic boulders, pushed downstream or rolled by an avalanche, were jammed into the ground at strange angles.

That place was neither on the topographical maps nor in Fausto's memories. Thirty years ago it was all glacier up there, and his father had taken him to see it. You could tell that the retreat had only recently taken place, because the boulders were not yet colonized by lichen and moss, and the sand had not become fertile ground yet, only a few pioneer weeds growing there. Fausto realized that he was observing a little piece of Earth that had just emerged into the sunlight, not yet named by man or marked on any of his maps.

A little farther up the old bivouac was still there, that

THE LOVERS

yellow metal half-barrel where he went to put down his rucksack. He didn't see anyone there. The last entry in the visitors' notebook had been three days earlier. The people had written: Fortunately, there are forgotten places! The whole space was occupied by six beds suspended from the walls and a little table in the center, plus a small pantry where it was customary to leave something for those who would come later. There was still time before he had to think about dinner. He changed his shirt and spread the sweaty one outside on the sheet metal warm from the sunlight, weighing it down with a stone so the wind wouldn't blow it away. Then he shut the bivouac door and went back down to the hollow.

Walking through the marsh he saw butterflies whose names he didn't know. Frogs had laid piles of their gelatinous eggs in the mud. He saw the snowfinches settling to drink and thought about how he remembered that place: the glacier's snout and the torrent that gushed from it mightily, the meltwater's metallic color. Once, with his father, they had started to calculate the flow rate and how much ice was melting per minute, hour, day, a volume that in the end seemed unlikely to Fausto. How could it melt at that pace and always stay the same? Back then he believed that the glacier was eternal and immutable, a part of the mountain he would always find there between rock and sky. His father, on the other hand, had understood what was happening: something disappears and something else will take its place, he told him. That's how the world works, you know? It's only us who miss what was there before.

It's really true, Papa, Fausto thought, and he used that place and the last hours of daylight to think about his father.

24

Two Hearts and a Hut

So Silvia saw him arrive at the refuge dusty and sweaty, with his sleeping bag rolled up on his rucksack and his green checkered shirt, rejuvenated and more beautiful than she remembered him. During the winter she didn't think of him as beautiful, just tormented, the way she liked her men. Now, though, he was beautiful: because of the summer, because he had walked for two days and slept in the bivouac, because he had managed in his little adventure to start out from Fontana Fredda and reach the Sella on foot. She kissed him instinctively, right there, among the mountaineers who were changing after their climbs up the four-thousanders. It was lunch hour, she didn't have time for pleasantries, but she kissed him for a full minute, with teeth, tongue, hands, and all. The climbers cheered.

Now that's a kiss, he said.

Where'd you disappear to? she said.

I've been working in the woods.

Really? You have to tell me all about it. Are you hungry?

Like a wolf.

Come inside.

By noon the refuge was bustling with people on their way in or out. Fausto recognized the lounge area, the period photos on the walls, the smell of cooking and sweat and old wood. Something else had changed from his childhood. They used to all be middle-aged men, speaking Italian or French or German, and each sign was translated into the three languages of Monte Rosa. Now it was full of young people, a variety you might find in the big cities of the world, and even the signs had been streamlined into English.

Silvia placed him at a table by the window, brought him a plate of tagliatelle alla fonduta and half a liter of wine.

I still have to work, she said, but I'll be with you in an hour.

Excellent. How's the chef?

He's Nepalese. A wizard with homemade pasta.

You're beautiful, you know that?

No, I'm not. My hair is gross.

Fausto ate while observing the people at the tables and the rope lines of climbers coming back from the glacier out the window. The climbers were half untied, limping, exultant, there were the exhibitionists and those exhausted by fatigue. One guy was throwing up behind the latrines. An old mountain guide in a red sweater and badge was coming back with three kids throwing snowballs at one another. There you go: you still see kids. He emptied a glass of wine, which at thirty-five hundred meters was worth double, it was barbera wine but had the effect of port. He saw Silvia serving a table across the room, returning to the kitchen, talking to a colleague of hers, then this other girl looked at him and smiled. He could guess the content of the conversation. He smiled back at her and made the gallant gesture of tipping his hat to her. Even Dufour, the famous guide passing by with three plates of pasta in his hands, recognized him.

Oh, he said, you made it.

Yeah, from home on foot.

Where's home?

Fontana Fredda.

No kidding! Must've had a lot of fuel.

I ran out of gas down below and had some trouble.

Eat, eat. There's more if you want.

Fausto wiped the remains of melted cheese with the bread and poured himself the last glass of wine, then leaned his back against the wall and relaxed. From the windows he could see the clouds gathering in the afternoon. The wine, the warmth of the refuge, the rising fog, the tired legs: he almost fell asleep sitting there. He closed his eyes and felt just like he used to. But now it was better than it used to be, because there were memories of him in between. That's what a refuge should be like, he thought. It's worth more if it's sheltering something of yours.

It was Silvia who rescued him from that half-sleep by grabbing him by the hand. She was finished with her shift and took him up to the bedroom, locked the door, undressed him. That way the lovers of Fontana Fredda could pick up where they'd left off at the end of winter. She found him leaner and more muscular, half-tanned and scented with resin. He found her gaunter and it brought out his tenderness. He felt like he had to take care of that body, which had been mistreated of late. Silvia let herself be caressed.

Later she said: I don't know how I'm doing. This place is incredibly beautiful. But it's so hard.

I believe it.

When I get off the cable car to get bread, I always stop to look at the little flowers below. You know those little flowers that grow on the moss, did you see them on the ridge?

I sure did.

But how do they grow at three thousand five hundred meters? And when I look at the valley it seems so green, so alive. You smell so good, like the woods.

She sniffed his neck and beard, and Fausto closed his eyes while she was sniffing. His pillow seemed to him the softest he'd ever put his head on. He said: You know, I felled my first tree this week.

Did you?

The loggers have taken a liking to me. Try it, chef! They gave me the most beautiful chain saw and the smallest plant, a poor little tree all crooked.

Did you manage?

Yeah, it's not hard.

And you liked cutting it down?

Not at all. I think I'm too delicate to become a highlander.

Why, you wanted to become a highlander?

Yeah, I did. Didn't you?

Silvia slipped her leg between his and pulled him to her. She clung to Fausto and twisted around him in her bossy way, as if he were a blanket to be pulled over her. He was so sleepy that he didn't resist.

She said: Sorry, I need human warmth.

Go for it.

I suffer from the cold too much to be a polar explorer.

Is that better?

A bit. Are you sleeping?

No, no.

But within a second Fausto was fast asleep. She wanted

to chat some more but he was snoring so calmly that it didn't matter after all. She nuzzled her forehead against his temple and closed her eyes. She was always tired, too. In the end they slept for two hours straight, while the fog rose outside, her with her gross hair and him smelling of sweat and sawdust and wine.

25

A Rescue

While the lovers were sleeping upstairs, a young man and woman came to the counter downstairs to ask for the manager. Dufour was checking the solar panel batteries because they wouldn't be getting any more sun that day, and in a while he would have to turn on the diesel generator. He dropped what he was doing there and listened to these kids, who had just come down from Castor. They told him that they had met a man all alone up at the summit. He was old, maybe about sixty, and he had told the two of them that he took that route every summer, he knew it by heart. For the young couple, though, it was the first time, they had just gotten married and were on their honeymoon, going from refuge to refuge. At the summit of Castor they joked a bit about marriage; the older man said he was envious because his wife hadn't been with him in the mountains for a while, and he complimented the woman on the pace at which he saw her climbing. He left shortly afterward. He said: We'll see each other again, you'll catch up to me on the way down. The two stayed for another quarter of an hour, ate a little, took a few photos of the peak, then moved on when they saw the mist rise. Actually, the fog had risen very quickly, already enveloping them on the ridge. In any case, the track was a highway and they had come down at a good pace, but they didn't run into the man again. They expected to find him in the refuge, but he wasn't there. Maybe he's gone already, the young man said. To which his wife added: Still, it's better we let you know, that's how you do it, right?

Yes, that's the way to do it, Dufour said. He wiped his hands on a rag and thought to himself: Here we go again.

He went to check the guest register from the night before: there were only two single bookings. One was a Dutchman, the other an Italian, whom he phoned, but the phone was off. There could have been various reasons, in theory; but in reality, not once did someone run away to Switzerland with their lover and throw their cell phone into a crevasse. He made some more phone calls; the couple was still there listening to him and he didn't feel like sending them away. He called the cable car station, he called the nearest refuge in case the man had come down from the wrong side in the fog, and he also called the helicopter, to be ready to go up at the first clearing. But he already knew that there would be no more clear weather that day. Finally he looked into the room. Among the people at the tables there was a young mountain guide, he was smart, fast. Dufour called the guide into the kitchen with the couple and Pasang, who was washing the pots. Dufour told him what he had just heard and asked the couple: How was he dressed?

I don't remember, the man said.

He's wearing a yellow windbreaker, the woman said. White hair and beard. A blue cap.

Try to go up, Dufour said. The helicopter can't take off right now, maybe it'll clear up soon.

Pasang and the guide set off like lightning in the soft afternoon snow. Dufour watched them disappear into the fog twenty meters from the refuge. He stayed in the kitchen, the only quiet and secluded place, in front of that window overlooking the glacier and the fog. Then all he could do was wait.

Sit down somewhere, he said to the couple. There's some tea.

If you ask me, he went down already, the young man said.

Could be. Let's hope so.

Shouldn't we call the mountain rescue?

Yeah, I'm the mountain rescue.

The young man was embarrassed. He sat down and didn't speak anymore. The young woman took two cups and filled them from the big pot of tea with the ladle.

While he waited, Dufour thought: Why would a sixty-year-old go alone along that ridge? But who was he? How come I never remember anyone?

So, honeymoon in the refuges, he said.

We've been thinking about it for so long, the young woman said.

Where have you been?

To the Gran Paradiso, then here. Next week we're going to the Dolomites.

That's right. A little sun. Enough ice, no?

He called that number back two more times but no answer. He checked the Swiss weather service, which gave overcast skies and low pressure until evening. People were coming into the lounge area and he thought he should reorganize the shifts. What was on the menu for dinner?

Three quarters of an hour passed when Pasang called on the radio. He said: Boss, there are tracks going down.

Where are you?

Halfway on the crest. You know where it turns?

Yes, it was always that point. It took Pasang and the guide three quarters of an hour to cover the trail that a good mountaineer did in double the time.

Which side does it go down, toward us or Switzerland?

Toward us.

Can you make out how far it goes down?

I can't see a thing.

Dufour was talking on the radio while looking out the window. He couldn't see anything either. Pasang's voice was coming from within that fog.

We'll try to go down, boss.

Do you have ice screws?

Yes, yes.

Be careful out there!

He didn't really need to tell him what to do: that Sherpa was the best guide he had ever met. He was precise, fast. He never lost his temper. And he was as strong as a mule. In Nepal, when they had first met, he would carry loads of eighty kilos on his back and find his way up and down the seracs around Everest by instinct. Dufour had said to himself: I'll take this one here to my refuge, he's worth gold.

Tracks? the woman said. But how come we didn't see any?

I was just trying not to get lost, the man said.

That's normal, Dufour said. You did well.

Pasang said: I made it to the rocks, boss.

Are the tracks still there?

They end here. I think he fell.

Can you get down there?

I'll try.

It wasn't like that slope was anything special, Dufour was walking it in his memory, looking for a spot where, with a little luck, the man might even have been stopped, with broken bones but alive. Though it wouldn't take much. You hit something wrong and that's the end of it.

Then Pasang said: I found him, boss. He's dead.

Where are you?

Down at the bottom of the rocks.

The young woman burst into tears. The young man turned pale. Dufour said: How do you know he's dead?

You can see.

How far is he from you?

Close. I'm above him.

Can you reach him?

I think so.

He waited with the radio in his hand, the woman sobbing in his ears. He'd made a mistake not to send them away. Their honeymoon was ruined. Then Pasang's voice said: I'm here, boss. He cracked his head on the rocks.

Pasang had seen so many deaths in the mountains, he was no longer impressed. Dufour also remembered the dead in the Himalayas, at the time of the eight-thousander fever: they had fallen or had stopped due to exhaustion, the cold preserved them and no one took them away.

What's the point of risking your life to bring a dead man down? He remembered a Japanese climber sitting on a boulder on the way up to Kangch. The wind kept him clear of the snow. Just a layer of frost on his face. He had been sitting there for a year or two.

Should I pull him up, boss?

How far down did he go?

Maybe two hundred meters. I can do it if you want.

Yes, without a doubt. Harnessing a corpse and dragging it up a two-hundred-meter slope: Pasang would have done it. Dufour thought of that lady, that wife who no longer went to the mountains with her husband. She must be at home, quiet for a few more minutes. What a shitty job, he thought. Why won't this whole glacier just melt once and for all? So we can get it over with.

He said: Is his backpack there?

Yes.

Look in the pockets. See if you can find any documents.

There's a wallet. A phone, too, but it's broken.

Take everything. Come on back.

Leave him here?

Yeah, leave him. We'll pick him up tomorrow in the helicopter.

Okay.

And be careful.

The radio went quiet and Dufour checked the time.

It was four in the afternoon. Now there were other things that needed to be done, aside from setting up dinner. More phone calls.

He said: You two get some rest. Did you need to go down? You can stay tonight as well if you want.

The young man said: Goddamnit, couldn't he have roped himself up to us? Why didn't we tell him?

You did well, the guide said.

The young woman was crying.

26

A Letter from Babette

It was the first letter Fausto had received in Fontana Fredda, and he stood there for a while and looked at his name and address on the white envelope. He went out to read it on the lawn in front of the house, it was an evening in late July, in the middle of haymaking. The baling hour, after the hay had been turned over and the afternoon sun had dried it well, and the scent pervaded the summer air.

The letter was written by hand and said:

Dear Fausto,

No, I'm not going back for now. The reason is that I'm fine where I am. The sea is green and

there's a black cormorant that's chosen the rock
down below as its home, I've been watching
him since this morning. I feel that sense of being
able to breathe that a new landscape can give
you, which I haven't felt for a long time. The
landscape you're used to gives you a different
sense, of familiarity, or of oppression at times,
but then in reality you don't even see it anymore,
unless you come back after being away or in the
eyes of a newcomer. Then you feel a little sadness
thinking back to the times when you were new,
too, and so were the eyes you looked with. Over
time everything becomes normal, the beautiful
parts and the ugly ones, the bad taste of humans
stops bothering you so much and the earth's
elegance only keeps you company.

And yet I also think that only those who get
used to it really see, because they've cleared
their eyes of any feelings. Feelings are colored
glasses, they trick your vision. Do you know that
Zen saying about mountains? It goes: "Before
I approached Zen, mountains for me were just
mountains, and rivers were just rivers. When I
started practicing, the mountains were no longer
mountains and the rivers were no longer rivers.
But when I reached clarity, the mountains went

back to being mountains and the rivers back
to rivers." I think you and I can understand
this story well, because that place is full of the
meanings we've given it. The meanings are
there among the fields, the woods, and the stone
houses. When the mountains meant freedom for
me, I saw freedom even in cows grazing! But the
mountain itself has no meaning, it's just a pile of
rocks over which water flows and grass grows.
Now, for me, it's gone back to being what it is.

And yet, and yet. You know, I'm glad you're
there now. Someone once told me that Fontana
Fredda had been a sad place before I arrived. No
one went there willingly, which gave the place a
sense of hostility and abandonment. And I had
put some kindness back into circulation. It was
nice to hear that, but at some point it became
another cage. If it wasn't for you! they'd say to
me. As if I had a duty to take care of Fontana
Fredda. I think your arrival relieved me. Because
I saw that you were in love. I'm still very fond
of Fontana Fredda and I know that whatever
happens I'll be leaving it in good hands.

Have you found another job? I'm sorry I
ditched you like this, but certain decisions are
made on instinct. Take care, dear Fausto: don't

drink too much, don't feel too guilty for the dead branches that fall in life, don't let that beautiful girl slip away. You're a very good cook, have I ever told you that? The best I've ever had.

Peace & Love,

Elisabetta/Babette

27

The Lost City

As for drinking and guilt, he still had some work to do, but he went back to Silvia throughout the summer. He was fit, he could climb up to her in less than two hours and run back down in one, so sometimes he would leave after work just to be with her in the evening, sleep together, and be back in the woods the next day. He really liked the idea of going to visit his girlfriend at the North Pole. The ticket seller at the cable car got used to seeing him arrive just before closing, with the climbers descending from the opposite cabin as he went up. Then the whole lift fell quiet and in the silence of the afternoon Fausto was left alone with the old trail, all the memories and meanings it had for him, the lakes that became mirrors in the waning light and the ibexes surprised to find a man at that hour. They rose from the rocks on which they were lying, a male snorted at him, and Fausto was already beyond the scree, already on the steps of the via ferrata with his big rucksack. If he hurried he might make it in time for the guides' aperitivo. He would always think of buying bread, a newspaper, fresh fruit and vegetables for the refuge workers, and of helping out in the kitchen if he saw they needed it. In the evening Arianna moved to another room. Dufour had long stopped making him pay the bill.

There was something contagious about the joy he brought up there, and one early morning Silvia let herself be persuaded to go for a walk on the glacier. They got ready at the back of the shelter, on that section of scree lit by the kitchen window. They put on their crampons and harnesses, tied themselves ten meters apart, and Fausto made some loops of rope that he wrapped around his shoulder. They set off just as it was getting light, and along Monte Rosa's trails the headlamps went out one by one.

But Fausto was no Pasang; he took off on his own race, and Silvia found herself having to keep up with him. For half an hour she just stared at the trail in the bluish snow and at the rope that bound her to him. At times the rope went taut and pulled her by the harness, other times it slackened too much and wound up in her crampons, and in neither case did Fausto turn around to check. It was as if, by tacit agreement, he would keep going forward and she would make sure that the rope between them stayed taut but not too much. Still, she was fine, well acclimatized to the high altitude. She didn't feel the cold, and the long, gentle rise beyond the shelter helped her find her rhythm. She barely noticed the two crevasses they passed, one by going around and the other by crossing a bridge of frozen snow. Her legs pumped with her heart and lungs, all in sync, and her breathing evened out.

Then it was Fausto who stopped to take off his rucksack. He took out an ice ax for himself and one for her.

You all right?

I think so, what do you say?

You're in good shape.

I must have gotten into shape washing floors.

Look, there's your refuge.

Silvia turned toward the valley: she saw Quintino Sella in the distance, the blue smoke from the generator, the windows illuminated in the morning mist. They'd passed some other rope lines. Now the slight slope was finished and they had a much steeper climb ahead. The whole cliff was still in the shade.

You want some tea?

Not now, thanks.

Shall we go right away?

Sure, I just got warmed up.

So: ice ax in the left hand and rope in the right. It's a bit rough here. Let's take it easy, okay?

Sure, I've seen your easy.

The trail on the rise turned out to be a succession of steps carved into the ice. They were high, reaching almost to Silvia's knee: her left foot rose, then her right foot followed. The ice ax, which would have been too short on a flat, was just right if you sank it in on the uphill side. Where the trail changed direction and turned left, Silvia imitated Fausto and passed the ice ax into the other hand. She figured out what the system was on her own. The trail zigzagged upward to tame that steep slope, and she remembered when, early in the season, Dufour or Pasang would go out to pack it down every time it snowed. Two guys pausing halfway up let them pass, the second bent over gasping for air; the first said: Next week the beach! Think of the girls in bikinis!

Yeah, but without you, the other said.

Silvia did not anticipate the sun that hit them at the end of that climb. The sun, the morning sky, and the horizon that suddenly opened in front of them, toward other glaciers and other peaks. They walked again, on the edge of the crest and then over a hump, descending on an unpredictably wide and peaceful plateau. Fausto stopped where the trail forked: one continued west toward Castor and the other east toward the two Lyskamm peaks. They were the famous crests that drew people from all over the world. A much larger glacier than the one they had just climbed descended on the opposite side of Monte Rosa, northward.

Is that the Felik Pass?

The one and only.

So we're already at four thousand?

Yeah, have been for a while. And here in front of us let me introduce his majesty, the Gorner Glacier. *Gornergletscher.*

It's immense. Where does it go?

Where does it go? Into the Rhône. And Lake Geneva. Then to Lyon and down into Provence.

Wow.

Here my father would always say to me: See if you can tell the difference between the snow of the Rhône and the snow of the Po. This watershed business always annoyed the shit out of him.

So that's where it was, the lost city of Felik. Silvia's first four-thousand-meter climb. Below them the valleys, barely touched by the sun, merged together, the blue planet wriggling back to life, and around them the surface of that frozen star shone. The Rosa crests looked like they had been cut with sword swipes. You could make out the ropes going up one by one. It was all so clear and essential that she began to understand Pasang's response in another way. Snow, wind, sun.

What time is it? she asked.

Seven. Time to go and make the cappuccinos.

Shall we go back down already?

Yeah, but now you lead.

I'd like to stay here a little longer.

Next time. For now remember: keep your weight back and plant your heels well.

Wait, Silvia said. And before planting her heels she kissed that despot at the head of her rope line on the mouth, with her crampons getting in the way and the rope tangling, there where the snow of the Rhône blended with that of the Po.

28

A Hangover

He called it the big cleaning, even though it was no longer spring. Seeing as how he'd had a fight with his daughter, how his daughter's mother was too stubborn to come back, how Fausto had gone up into the mountains, leaving him alone, and how he was still struggling to tie his shoes four months after the accident, he decided to resort to his dear old bulldozer method, the thought crusher. He started with a cup half full of gin and the other half Fontana Fredda water, that holy water that came straight from the glacier, then continued throughout that August afternoon, gradually losing his sense of time and dosage: sometimes it was more water, sometimes more gin, but it still had that good juniper flavor and went down cleansing his soul of rust and crust. Ex-husband, ex–forest ranger, now probably an ex–snowcat driver as well, with two good-for-nothing hands and fat clogging his veins, the gin cleaned everything away for Luigi Erasmo Balma, also known as Santorso, like the ancient Irish monk. It was said that the man had come down from his green island to become a hermit among the mountain dwellers. A hermit, why not? He looked out the window and saw that if he raised the cup to the right height he could see the mountains reflected upside down in the gin. After another refill, the perspective on his situation also began to change. Looking at them in the gin, all those exes became steps toward a liberation. Free from a marriage, a uniform, a salaried job, he'd get by anyway, give me a chain saw and a potato field and I'll make do. His good, judicious daughter had cut out his cigarettes but she wasn't aware of the Toscano cigar he kept in a drawer, and this seemed to him just the right opportunity. The liberation of Santorso, patron saint of hermits. Give me a cave, a *barma*, I'll build the dry stone wall myself. He took a drag from the Toscano and the savor of tobacco mixed with the juniper in his mouth.

That was when he saw his black grouse again embalmed and hung on the wall. He set the cup aside, pulled the grouse down, and walked out into the afternoon sun. On the road tourists were returning from their hike, the children played among the round bales in the field. Santorso still managed to grip a hammer; he nailed the bird to the trunk of the larch in front of the house. He went back in and up onto the balcony to evaluate his work, cup in hand again and the Toscano between his teeth. There you go, free, fly, blackcock, go fight with some bully from the valley next door, find a nice little grayhen and make lots of chicks. Who knows why in thirty years he had never thought about freeing him, it seemed so right now, hanging him out there. Down at the end of the meadow a few blond girls passed by in tank tops. Where were they going, without even saying hi? Had it not been for the blondes, the next idea wouldn't have come to him. Oh no, he thought, you're not free. You'll always be nailed to your *brenga*. Just like this old cock here.

He went back inside, then to the cowshed, and came out again with the twelve-gauge. Over-under barrel, buckshot cartridges. Let's see if I'm still good, he thought, opening and closing his right hand to stretch his fingers. Hey, blackcock, you remember this? Still the same as last time, eh. He picked up the shotgun and thankfully one eye had to be closed to take aim, so instead of two grouse only one was left. His right index finger managed to squeeze what he had to squeeze. Boom! went the twelve-gauge. Boom! Two shots in the middle of August heard all the way down to Tre Villaggi, and the terrified mothers ran to gather their children out of the meadows.

29

A Pile of Stones

Two women arrived at Quintino Sella a few days after mid-August. They had hired a guide to accompany them and climbed slowly, taking a whole morning and part of the afternoon. They had no peaks planned, they just wanted to get there. At the refuge they dismissed the guide, who ran off to take the last cable car, and went to look for their places in the dormitory. On the phone they had asked if there were double rooms with bathrooms, one of those questions, not even the most ridiculous, that people laughed about in the kitchen. But the two women adjusted to the bunk bed, spread out the sheet and blanket, and went back to the lounge to drink tea. One had gray hair tied up and wore a crew-neck sweater; the other, holding the cup in her hands to keep warm, was blond and wore earrings that clashed with the refuge's rubber slippers. Silvia noticed them as soon as she went downstairs. Who are those two? she thought. Then she yawned, tied her apron, and said: Ciao, Friday.

Ciao, Woman of the Woods.

What are we eating tonight?

Pasta with tomato sauce or vegetable puree soup. Second course is stew with mashed potatoes or spinach pie.

When will you make us *dal bhat*?

In September!

Everything in September, eh?

The refuge was packed and there was a double shift at dinner, half past six and half past seven, and she didn't have time to breathe until nine. Then the climbers' stomachs became sated and the work finally slowed down. Some went out to look at the glacier and the stars, others played cards while drinking a nightcap, a few insisted on checking the equipment for the next day. Then Silvia noticed the two women again: Dufour was now at the table with them, explaining something with the help of a map. She had never seen him sit with anyone other than a mountain guide, so who could those two be? The gray-haired woman seemed more involved in the conversation. The blonde was leafing through the visitors' notebook; she had red eyes and an absent air. Then at one moment Silvia understood. A month had passed since that day, hundreds or thousands of climbers, but she knew there was nothing in the notebook to read, the Castor man hadn't even left his signature. There were those who filled entire pages and those who passed though in silence, as if not wanting to disturb. Dufour stood talking to them while Silvia set the tables for breakfast, then it was time to turn off the generator and send everyone to bed.

The wife is the blond one, Arianna told her up in the room. The other is a friend.

Is it always like this when someone dies?

Almost always. Sooner or later a wife or child arrives. It's sadder when the parents arrive.

Your father is good.

He had to learn.

When my mom died, the priest came. I didn't even want to see him.

She went to church?

You must be kidding, she hated that guy. She said the Church was unfair competition.

So you did well.

The next morning was calm and clear, high pressure in August. No wind, even the glacier managed to look like an earthly place. The two women had breakfast and then went out to look at the peaks and the ropes already far away. The blonde wandered around the refuge, she looked at the old lodge and bronze plaques, the glacier birds and Tibetan flags, as if looking for something she couldn't find. Her friend was sitting on a bench in the sun when Silvia came out of the latrines with the bucket and rag.

Hello, the woman with gray hair said.

Good morning.

The view is incredible from up here.

It is.

What's that glittering down there?

They told me it's a factory in Novara. It always glitters at this time of the morning. If there were no haze, you could see Milan a little farther down.

Milan?

Silvia put down the bucket to point it out to the woman. By now she knew what made an impression on people: there were those who looked up and those who looked down.

Do you see the mountains over there? That one on its own is Monviso, over there is Turin. And that light blue line isn't haze, it's the Ligurian Apennines. Behind them is the sea.

The sea.

It's strange, isn't it? To think of the sea up here?

The woman took a better look at her. She seemed to realize only now that she was talking to little more than a girl. This, too, had already happened to Silvia.

You could serve them at the table for an entire evening without them seeing you, you were just the waitress who brought them food, then sometimes with a word, a gesture, they suddenly put you in a different light.

How old are you?

Almost twenty-eight.

Have you been working here long?

Since June. It's my first summer.

You're brave.

Silvia picked up the bucket. She laughed to herself. Yes, you had to be brave to enter the latrines after one hundred and twenty climbers had passed through, most of them with stomachaches. At first she also saw it this way, she hadn't understood much about life in the refuge.

The arrival of the blond woman put an end to the conversation. She wore a pair of dark glasses, good for the glacier and for mourning, and Silvia made as if to go and leave them alone. But it was the blonde who stopped her and said: Excuse me.

Yes?

I was wondering what those piles of stones were. Do they mean anything?

Yes and no.

How's that?

The tallest was built by a Nepalese man who works

here. It's a kind of Buddhist altar, you hang prayer flags
from it.

Is that what those tattered cloths are?

Yes, but it's not a problem that they're tattered, not at
all. For them it's the prayers that fall apart in the wind.

And the smaller piles?

Those are made by people passing through, I don't
know why.

They do it just to do it?

Silvia shrugged. She said: You know, afternoons are
long. Maybe it's just a way to pass the time. Or maybe to
say: I've been here, too.

She realized she was starting to speak like Pasang. She
wished she had something nice to add, a word for that
woman. But the truth was that she didn't remember her
husband. She had tried, she had gone over all the faces of
that evening, but the next day other faces had arrived and
the accident had quickly ended up in the catalogue, they
happened all the time. Some so bizarre that a simple fall
into the fog wouldn't be talked about for long.

Are you a Buddhist? the gray-haired woman asked.

Me, no. I only have this friend.

Then she said: If you'll excuse me, I have to go work.

Later she saw them out there building their pile. Two
women gathering stones from the scree and stacking them
one on top of the other. Only they knew the meaning.

It took them half the morning and became a beautiful pile nearly a meter high, solid enough that it might withstand the winter. Silvia saw them again while they were trying to pay the bill, Dufour didn't want any money but accepted the tip for the staff, then at around eleven the guide arrived to take them back down.

30

The Bivouac

Fausto's father used to tell him that mountain torrents have five voices, which change with the hours
of the day. Now the third voice, the powerful one in the
afternoon, was fading into the fourth, and at sunset the
torrent subsided as if a floodgate had been lowered up-
stream. In the basin at the foot of the glacier you could
hear the coming autumn. In August the cottongrass
had blossomed, there was a stretch of it on the marsh:
white tufts hanging from stalks that grew in the stagnant
water and swayed in the three-thousand-meter wind like
a cotton field.

In that sheet-metal half-barrel Fausto lit the camping
stove; he chopped the onion with his Opinel knife while
the dried mushrooms soaked in the warm water. Rice,
broth powder, mountain toma cheese, and a bottle of

Nebbiolo also came out of his backpack. Silvia watched him from the bed above, drinking the wine. They'd arranged a date there, with her coming down from the perennial winter of the refuge and him going up from the short summer of Fontana Fredda, or what was left of it.

Don't you ever get tired of cooking?

No. Actually, it's very relaxing. Helps me focus.

Why, are you usually anxious?

Not anxious. A bit worried.

About work?

That, too. Must be the fall mood. Whether to write or not, what to do next winter.

You say Babette won't reopen?

I don't think so.

Have you written anything these days?

A little, yeah.

And cooking keeps you focused on me, or only on the onions and mushrooms?

On the onions and mushrooms and you.

Okay, then. Could you pour me some more wine?

They had dinner as it was getting dark outside. In the last light the chamois came down from their cliffs and ridges to drink. They kept away from the bivouac, passing wider than the usual route. They also knew the fall mood: the grass was losing its flavor, and at any moment they would hear the first gunshots. Man became very dangerous in that season.

Fausto opened his backpack and took out a crumpled package. He said: Happy birthday. Sorry for the bow.

Oh, chef! I wasn't expecting this.

Better that way.

What could it be?

Wild mountain flowers. Go ahead, open it.

From out of the wrapping paper came one of the black notebooks in which Fausto had been writing. On the front page it carried the title *Thirty-Six Views of Fontana Fredda*. And then the dedication: *To my polar explorer, with love, F.* There followed short chapters written in longhand, with a penmanship that struggled to be legible. Silvia leafed through a few pages: one spoke of a tree struck by lightning, one of a late snowfall, one of felling trees, and so on.

You really did write.

That's because I can't draw.

But are you sure it's for me?

Of course it's for you. It's one of a kind.

I don't know if I deserve it.

What about me, do I deserve a kiss?

Who knows why they always had to do it in the cold? The bivouac was tight and uncomfortable but it had certainly seen other lovers in its long life. Always half dressed, sunburned, with tired legs and dirty hair and too many smells on them: bivouac and refuge lovers. It got dark in the basin and the temperature dropped a few degrees. Only the rock gave off the heat it had soaked up, warm in the night air.

How did that story go about the bivouac blown away by the wind? she said.

Like this. Once upon a time there was a little bivouac, just like this one. Some guy went away in the fall, left the door open, and in the spring only the concrete base was left. That's my story.

That's not true.

What are you doing in the fall?

In October I've got the apple harvest.

That's right, it's apple season.

Then I don't know. I'm twenty-eight, I should decide what to do in life.

And if we were to look for a place we could run together, you and me? Wouldn't you like that?

A refuge?

I've been thinking about it for a while.

Let's hear.

I cook. You deal with the counter. A little place, working together, just the two of us.

The cook and the waitress?

Why not?

You are just too romantic.

Bivouac lovers: he was too romantic, she had to decide what to do in life, and they talked about it from a suspended cot that wasn't even a bed, inside a shack at the mercy of the elements. Still, it was true that Fausto had been thinking about it for a while. He had put his idea together carefully; now he was already talking to her about vacant refuges, refuges closed for years, refuges off the beaten track, small refuges at lower altitudes he knew. They could make a company, the two of them, and reopen one. By now they had learned the trade, hadn't they? It might not have been a marriage proposal, but it wasn't far off.

Cuddled up against him on her side, under a sleeping bag that barely covered them both, Silvia listened. There he was, running out ahead of her again. It was like that time on the glacier, when he took the lead without turning around and the rope kept tugging her harness. But the evening was too perfect to ruin with objections. She imagined she was listening to a fairy tale, or one of his typical boy-and-girl stories, and before it was over she fell asleep.

31

Avalanche Fences

Overnight there had been a storm and in the morning the glass he had left on the balcony contained a fly drowned in two finger-widths of water. He looked over at the fields, drinking the light coffee his daughter had made: the straw-colored grass, the sky clear and hazeless again. The light was changing, he thought. Time to get cracking and chop some wood. Then he heard the bathroom door open and she walked out in her white shirt, black pants, the hotel badge on her breast pocket, her hair pulled back into a flawless bun.

You work on Sundays, too? Santorso asked.

Sunday, Monday, what's the difference. What are your plans?

I guess I'll sharpen the chain saw.

No hunting today?

Do they make you keep your hair back like that? You have such beautiful hair, set it free a little.

You're supposed to say let your hair down. I'm going.

Bye, baby.

He watched her get into the car, back out, and disappear around the first bend, driving slowly, keeping well to the right, toward her hotel with a swimming pool. But whose daughter was that girl? Then he took his backpack and binoculars and went out too. He set off on the path from which the loggers had come down just a few days earlier. Once the logging site was dismantled, the wood was luminous: branches piled up at the base of the larches, stacks of logs sorted by quality. After a rainy night, steam rose up from them in the morning sun. He passed the stretch of shavings, the blackened stones on which Fausto had cooked, the farm where he passed a herder's van. The man stopped and with his elbow out the window asked him: You going up to Valnera?

If I can manage.

Can you keep an eye out for my steers?

You got 'em up there?

I got twenty-two of 'em. I'm hoping the storm didn't scare 'em.

Okay.

And while you're up there, why don't you shoot me a chicken for lunch?

Go fuck yourself.

Above the woods he found the stream thinner, all stones and gravel at the bottom, and the grass turning greener to compensate. He still wasn't used to the new pace his aches and pains forced him to take. He couldn't maintain the pace he had kept all his life, if he went faster he immediately got out of breath, and a couple of times he said to himself, Listen, forget it, go back down and sharpen the chain saw. But he hung tough. For an hour he just stared at the trail under his feet. He realized he was already pretty high up when he saw the withered gentians in the grass. He thought: With these itty-bitty strides I might even wind up reaching the Margherita hut. They'll say, Look at that old man making his way up, slow as a lawn mower but he's got a good rhythm.

At the edge of the Valnera he was greeted by marmots trilling. Where the stream formed a pond, he found that ballbreaker's steers drinking. They were heifers, actually, females a year or two old who had no milk and were left in the high pastures throughout August and September, in a half-wild state. At first they were afraid, wary of anything passing by. After a month you found them wild, at times they would charge, and getting them to obey could get complicated. Santorso counted them: thirteen. They must have gotten separated during the storm. He went up through the meager pastures where the valley ended, little more than a hillside; whereas the other end fell into crags and cliffs and it was there that a few years earlier they had put up all those avalanche fences, after the houses below had been strafed by stray stones from the rockslides. They looked like open umbrellas placed upside down. That was the site of his accident, but going back there left him neither hot nor cold. For him it was like he'd fallen down the stairs in his house.

He found the spot where he'd lost his skis and started looking: one was on the scree, the sealskin in shreds, but the ski itself along with the binding was still in good condition. The other had fallen, most likely below. He leaned out over the other drop and looked down.

Dio faus, he said out loud.

The nine heifers were there, or at least their carrion among the murder of crows. Some were stuck in the avalanche fence, torn from hindquarters to chest. They were half-eaten meals: when the best parts were finished, they were left to the birds now crowding around their snouts, pecking inside their open bellies. They still had their collars and cowbells, their yellow ear tags, some with stiff legs in the air and tongues sticking out. Even in death they kept their awkwardness, out of place in that terrain which was not for cows, but for chamois and ibexes. And now wolves as well.

Young wolves, Santorso thought. It's the young ones who kill for fun, the old ones only when hungry. This was no longer a lone hunter but a pack that had methodically separated the heifers, pushed them up the slope and then down the cliff. While chasing them they snapped at their flanks, hindquarters, udders; they made an easy game of it with those beasts that no longer knew how to defend themselves or flee, domesticated animals in the wild. The wolf cubs must have enjoyed themselves like crazy, then they ate their fill and finally went off to digest somewhere else.

It would take a few nice helicopter rides to clean up that cull, but Santorso was in no hurry to call the forestry department. They had a good laugh when they confiscated his rifle, did they? Well, fuck them. Now he saw the second ski next to one of the carcasses, it had fallen down there and an avalanche fence had stopped it. He climbed down slowly, clinging to the tufts of hard grass, down the same gully where that volley of stones had hit him. He trusted his hands and his hands did not betray him, and the crows rose up around him to protest the invasion.

32

The Apple Harvest

Forget the orchards and vineyards, Silvia knew she had arrived when she saw the factory wall pass by from the train window. That yellow, peeling paint, behind which her grandfather had worked for a lifetime, and her father until production was moved abroad. After it shut down, somebody with a spray can had written GOODBYE FUCK YOU BUT WAIT FOR ME, probably not to the factory but to some lover who was taking the train, and since then it had always been Silvia's welcome back home. She took her earbuds out and the song she was listening to was cut short.

This is where I get off, she said to the boy sitting next to her.

Okay, bye.

Thanks for the music.

No problem.

She pulled her rucksack down from the overhead rack, proceeded through the aisle, and got out among the students and commuters. She was struck by the mild September evening, she saw sandals and bare shoulders whereas only a few hours earlier she was traipsing through snow. She thought she would come down from the glacier on foot and say goodbye slowly, but that morning the helicopter was carrying the trash down and Dufour was having one of those days when there was no time for discussion, busy as he was with all the end-of-season tasks. Then he pointed to her and Arianna, and said: On the next trip, you two go down, and ten minutes later Silvia was in the parking lot of the cable car. Suddenly no more glacier, she felt as if she had been tricked. She exchanged phone numbers with Arianna and half a promise to take a trip together in the spring.

She walked out of the station, a polar explorer who at every intersection was forced to say to herself: Watch out, that's a traffic light. It's red, can't you see? And those are pedestrian crossings. Now her refuge was the rucksack she was carrying, and her best friends those feet in their boots. Feet that had learned an art up there, made of toes, heels, ankles, arches, feet that had become deft acrobats on rock and ice, and now back on asphalt proved to be a much less efficient means of locomotion than the wheel. This was the neighborhood. Here were the two bars in the square, the drug dealers' benches, here the jobless drinking Campari and white wine, here the youth center where for a while she committed herself to making her neighborhood a little better. With the change of administration it was assigned to others and now they watched the ball games inside. Where were the flowers in this glacier? And yet there had to be flowers here, too.

What are you doing in the fall, Friday?

I'm going to Nepal for the trekking season, then I'll stay home with my family for a while. And you?

Yeah, I think I'll go home for a while too.

She had returned because she felt ready, after an escape that seemed very long to her. She would say this to Fausto: that before going forward she had to go back, otherwise she would always be someone running away. Hence the buildings, the balconies, the courtyards in between, the ramps going down to the garages that as children they weren't allowed on, the bike frames with no wheels and the garbage bags that still stank. Hence the polar explorer rediscovering her whole childhood with moist eyes, and her childhood astonished to find her again.

Little Silvia! an old lady said as she hung her laundry on the floor above.

Ciao, Melina.

I haven't seen you for ages, are you back?

Yeah, for a while.

Where are you coming from with that pack?

From the mountains.

Must be nice and cool.

Pretty much.

Remember to say hello to your father for me.

I sure will.

She took the stairs instead of the elevator, and the fifth-floor apartment was her last summit for that year. Five floors, one hundred and twenty steps, seventeen meters difference of altitude, give or take. Her legs had gotten strong and it would have been a shame to forgo the workout. The polar explorer approached the door, the door to what was now her father's house, and then she thought of the Felik, the sword-cut ridges and the glacier descending beyond. Fausto saying, Now try to distinguish the snow of the Rhône from that of the Po, if you can. She summoned that memory to give her the courage she needed. Then she rang the bell, tucked her hair behind her ear, and smiled at the peephole like a little girl in a photo booth.

33

The Potato Field

Fausto had the insomnia of a man who has to make a decision. He listened to the drizzle on the roof, closed his eyes, and may have fallen asleep for a few moments, but at first light he got tired of tossing and turning, stepped out of bed, and loaded the stove with dry twigs. Fine drops were falling outside, clouds covered the woods, and the kitchen filled with smoke from the low pressure. Half an hour later he went back to the window and saw snow as the clouds cleared. There it was: settling above two thousand meters, September snow that would soon melt in the sun, but it was there. He tried to remember the last spring snowfall, it must have been the beginning of June, a little over three months between one and the other. Just as Santorso had once told him: three months of cold, nine of freezing. The time for jaunts was over, he thought, now was the time for the stove, for wisdom and plans about how to spend the coming winter, so he decided to go down to the local branch of the bank.

At Tre Villaggi there was only one employee, who opened the counter twice a week. He was kind and patient and gave Fausto all the information on short-term loans, then he asked him a few questions about income, assets, and guarantees he could offer. Fausto had no guarantees. The clerk checked his balance, raised an eyebrow in front of the screen, jotted down a chart of installments and interest on a sheet of paper, asked him for his identity card to make a photocopy. Fausto was ashamed of the word he'd had put on it, *writer. Cook* would have been much better for the bank. In the end, the amount they could lend him, without making too much of a fuss, was fifteen thousand euros to be repaid in five years; plus what he had in his account made twenty-seven thousand. He would go into debt again, but at least he could afford to start a business without gasping for air. He came out of the bank more cheerful than he had entered. Fausto was still a writer who as soon as he saw money, or rather the possibility of money, wanted to spend it, so he went to the hardware store to treat himself to a gift. He bought a new ax with an ash handle and a heavy splitting blade. It wasn't even eleven yet when he got back to Fontana Fredda; the clouds were rising in fraying shreds and up above, beyond the rain-damp woods, they revealed pastures covered by that finger-width of snow.

Gemma was in the potato field checking out her plants. Fausto sat down on the side of the road and said: Ciao, Gemma.

Good morning.

You like the snow?

Me, no. I've seen too much of it.

But we need it, don't we?

We need it in December. In September it's only a nuisance.

How do the cows up in the mountain pastures manage?

They don't go out in the snow. For today they'll be eating hay.

I didn't know that.

He would have liked to ask her: Gemma, what do you think, is it a good idea for me to take out a fifteen-thousand-euro loan so I can take over a restaurant that's losing money? If I do the cooking, that way hiring one less person, and raise the prices a bit, can I make it happen? Will they go for an extra euro on the workers' menu?

Instead he said: And how are the *trifolle* doing?

You speak dialect?

Two or three words.

A writer who speaks dialect!

So then you know who I am.

Gemma didn't answer. She looked down and stroked the leaves of a potato plant, as if wiping the rain off. To take her out of her embarrassment Fausto said: Listen, do you have any wood? Look at this beautiful ax I bought.

Beautiful.

If you want, I'll bring you a couple of wheelbarrows. I've got plenty.

It wasn't true or at least not entirely, because Gemma's fireplace wasn't smoking that morning. She must have had another hide to get through a day like that without lighting up the stove. He decided that he would bring the wood to her anyway, and he got up and went off to play with his new ax.

34

A Rekindling

And so you missed the summer, she told herself as she arrived on the small plateau. Fontana Fredda's was no summer, more like a spring that faded into autumn at its peak. You knew when it was happening because the snow up above that gave water to the torrents disappeared, and the meadow grass turned yellow right after. Babette had missed the June blossoms, though she had waited for them with devotion for thirty-five years. Now all that was left of the bluebells, dandelions, forget-me-nots, and yarrow were mown and fertilized fields, and of the willow herbs just dry stems on the banks. She opened the door to the restaurant and found it as she had left it in the winter: even the cups in the sink, the last orders hanging next to the counter, and her familiar disorder, which she would try to remedy from time to time. In the end disorder always won, her tendency to scatter things around her, to transform them from useful objects to objects that kept her company. She placed two sets of keys and the envelope with the contract on a table. She turned on the lights, the radio, the coffee machine, and the restaurant came to life. She filled a jug of water and went out to try and work the same miracle with the poor plants on the terrace. In six months no one had thought of watering them a little. As she bathed the roses and bluebonnets, she observed the closed cottages, the chairlift seats swinging in the wind, the smoke from the chimneys up in the mountain pastures, and the snow-streaked ridges on the horizon. Karen Blixen came to mind, not for *Babette's Feast* but for *Out of Africa*, where she had written: *If I know a song of Africa, of the giraffe and the African new moon lying on her back, of the plows in the fields and the sweaty faces of the coffee pickers, does Africa know a song of me?* And did Fontana Fredda know a song about her?

It took Santorso less than a quarter of an hour to notice her return. He walked up the stairs to the terrace limping slightly. He said: Is it open?

No.

Not even for a coffee?

I'll offer you a coffee. But the bar is closed.

So I'll sit here?

Why, you wanted to come in?

No, no, it's fine even outside.

Sit down. The machine is warming up. Be patient.

I'm in no hurry.

Santorso sat down at one of the plastic tables, next to the closed umbrella. When Babette walked back into the restaurant he couldn't help but look at her ass. That ass that thirty-five years ago, as soon as it got off the bus, had turned the whole valley upside down. He found it more solid than in the winter, and peering through the window he noticed that she also had a more relaxed face. The freckles had reappeared on her skin. How long had he not seen them, maybe since summers in the mountain pastures? With that white skin and red hair she burned herself every time she went out to the meadows. In those last months he often wondered if she had found a man where she had gone, and now as he watched her washing the cups, he kept looking for signs of something new. Let's see, old copper, if you can still spot a woman in love. Babette opened the water faucet, forgot about it, went to write a note to herself on a piece of paper; she made a shot of espresso with an empty portafilter to clean out the machine and then noticed the faucet as if someone else had opened it. Santorso still had some doubt about her being in love. He had a better under-standing of the ptarmigan and ermine. Finally she came out with two coffees, a glass of water, and a bottle of brandy; she put the tray on the table and sat down op-posite him.

Ciao, Luigi.

Ciao, Betta.

I heard you weren't doing so good.

They told you?

Yeah. How's it going now?

Slowly slowly.

Slowly slowly better?

Yeah, I guess.

He opened and closed his hands into fists. He didn't show her the two fingers that had set crooked. She put sugar in her coffee and he poured a dash of brandy into his. Everything just as it once was: they were an old couple sitting at an outdoor table at a mountain café in low season. He tried to find something nice to say, and said: We missed you at haymaking.

Hay? Must be ten years since I've done that.

Ten years? Time sure does fly.

How was the hay?

Crap. Yellow-rattles all over. If you don't cut it before the seeds come out, it'll get worse next year.

So you cut it early?

Yeah, but it won't do any good if I'm the only one.

How come?

Seeds fly.

I get it. Try and convince them to cut the hay early.

You got it.

She drank the water before the coffee. Who knows where she got that habit? he wondered. In Greece, in Spain? Where was it they drink water with coffee? He emptied his and then poured another finger of brandy to clean the cup, but he didn't take out his cigarettes and she noticed that. Had he quit smoking? So he wasn't completely crazy.

He said: Did you know the wolves are back?

So it's true?

Yeah, and a lot of them.

They should let the wolves take this place back. Don't you think? Anyway, there's no one here anymore.

Is it true you're giving the restaurant away?

I'm not giving it away, I'm giving over the management.

To Faus?

You know everything already.

And what are you gonna do?

I'll open a flower shop.

Santorso looked at her. He saw that blush he knew well under the freckles. Years ago he had married a girl unable to lie. That's a lie, he said. Babette burst out laughing.

God, he thought, when she laughed she was seventeen again. He was about to say: Can I kiss you? But she got up, left him the bottle and the little cup, and went back to her restaurant, messing the place up a little more before giving it away.

35

The Wood Auction

In October the forest was blooming with the yellow of larches and the red of fly agaric. Barely a trace of that intoxicating summer scent remained under the smell of mushrooms, musk, and withered grass. The stacks of logs had been measured and numbered, five cubic meters each, each with its number painted on the largest log. They went from one to more than two hundred, but on the morning of the auction only six people showed up. One was the farmer whose cows got mauled by the wolves. He was having a discussion with the forest ranger who was there to make sure everything was on the level.

If they're attacking me, tell me why I can't attack them?

They're not attacking you. They're attacking the livestock.

Same thing.

It's not the same thing. Anyway, I'm not the one who decides. It's a protected species. Just take the compensation and that's that.

Compensation! I'll get myself a cup of coffee with the compensation!

C'mon now, it's not the wolves that are the problem.

At nine o'clock the clerk decided that they could begin. She started from stack number one, which went unsold. Two and three also unsold. The starting price was set at one hundred euros per stack. She asked: Any bidders for number four? But in the first thirty or forty there was some Scotch pine inside that nobody wanted. It was crooked, resinous wood, it crusted up the pipes, and with all that abundance it was better to take the larch, which burned better. So the clerk had to go up a long stretch of the path calling numbers out to nobody.

For Fausto it was like retracing the days of summer. Now that they were walking around in heavy jackets, it was hard to believe it had been hot up there. Hard to believe the heat and weightlessness of July: the open fires, his hands smeared with resin, the fox rummaging through the potato skins, the loggers' hair full of sawdust. *Ciao, chef!* And then him running to get to Silvia's refuge. The clerk's question became a chant. Any bids for number forty-two? Any bids for number forty-three?

A whole summer of work, and now all that wood wasn't worth twenty euros per cubic meter.

So what are you going to call it? Santorso asked. Dio Faus?

No, no. The name stays Babette's Feast.

Even without Babette?

I'll be Babette.

And your girl, is she coming to work with you?

Fausto gently kicked a mushroom someone had picked up and left upside down. Never understood why they did that. Some days earlier he had spoken to Silvia on the phone, but the reaction wasn't what he expected.

I guess if she's into it.

Why? She's not into it?

Go figure what other people want.

You're telling me.

They worked their way up to the farm road and there the desires of the mountain men were awakened. Any bids for number fifty-seven? Me, said one. Does anybody raise the offer? Nobody. It wasn't a real auction because they had already agreed among them. Each one bought the five stacks to which he was entitled at the starting price, at the spot easiest to reach by tractor. Santorso bought his higher up, in the sun, where the growth rings of the larch dwindled and the wood was red and hard, and Fausto took lot 108 because he liked the number.

He looked sad to Santorso. You're only taking one?

Yeah, I guess.

Take four, go ahead.

And what'll I do with them?

Cut and split, we can sell it for a good price. I'll help you. That way we can work a little before the winter.

If you say so.

He took five, from 108 to 112. It gave him a strange feeling to think that he owned trees, even though they were no longer trees, actually, but only stacked logs. The clerk gave him a note so he could go down to the town hall and pay, after which the auction was declared finished. More than one hundred and seventy stacks remained unsold, which some large company would take away at a discounted price in the spring.

36

The Larches

I don't know if I want to spend another winter as a
waitress for skiers, she said. That wasn't how you were
talking about it.

It's something, he said.

If it's just to do something, I can pour drafts of beer
here at the neighborhood pub.

It's not Fontana Fredda.

Look, I've got no connection with Fontana Fredda.

And with me?

Silvia didn't answer. A month on the plain, and her
voice was already coming from very far away. Other
times Fausto had noticed, even with himself, that you
thought of the mountains one way when you lived there,
and in another when you were away from them. From
a distance, the reality faded into an idea: the woods,

houses, fields, streams, animals, and men became a triangle with snow on top, Mount Fuji on the horizon in Hokusai's drawings.

I want to spend some time with my father, Silvia said.

Sure, I understand.

What's it like there now?

It's quiet. You know what's sad when fall comes? You don't hear the cowbells anymore.

So what's there to do in October in Fontana Fredda?

You cut wood. Hopefully the water in the fountains won't run out. You harvest potatoes. I helped Gemma the other day, we must've pulled out a couple hundred kilos.

Who's Gemma?

My neighbor, don't you remember?

I don't think so.

It was just like that: the reality of Fontana Fredda vanished quickly in her. They talked some more about the restaurant, the staff to be hired and the opening date, and Silvia concluded that she would think about it a few more days.

I might be able to come up for two weeks at Christmastime. I don't have to stay all winter. I'll come up to help you.

Sure.

Don't be mad, c'mon.

Don't worry.

What are you cooking up tonight that's good?

I don't like to cook for myself. Maybe a couple of eggs.

You mean a lot to me, chef.

You mean a lot to me, too.

Fausto hung up shortly after. There on the balcony where he stood, he missed her voice immediately. He looked at the woods and noticed that the outermost branches of the larches were beginning to turn yellow. They were the trees of Fontana Fredda, trees of the sun, of the wind, of the southern slopes, but they didn't like frost and when they felt it coming they went into hibernation. The fir trees, impassive, kept their needles and wasted no energy in the seasonal molt: two trees so close together, and two very different strategies for facing the winter. Now the first to wither were the larches that had been wounded, some by lightning, some by a rockslide, some by a dig that had cut a root, then in a few days the whole wood would turn yellow and red, retreating into a long sleep while the dark green of the firs stood guard.

Somewhere Fausto had read that trees, unlike animals, cannot seek happiness by moving elsewhere. A tree lived where its seed had fallen, and to be happy it had to make do there. It solved its problems on the spot, if it was capable, and if not, it died. Whereas the happiness of herbivores followed the grass, in Fontana Fredda it was a glaring truth: March on the valley floor, May in the pastures at a thousand meters, August in the mountain pastures around two thousand, and then back down

to the lesser happiness of autumn, the second modest
flowering. The wolf obeyed a less fathomable instinct.
Santorso had told him that no one knew exactly why the
wolf moved, the source of his restlessness. He arrived in
a valley, maybe found plenty of game, yet something pre-
vented him from staying put, and at a certain point he left
all that bounty there and went to seek happiness somewhere else. Always through new woods, always beyond
the next ridge, chasing the scent of a female or the howl
of a pack or nothing so evident, carrying away with him
a song of the younger world, as Jack London wrote.

Anyway, Fausto was not the type to wallow too much
in self-pity. Silvia might come up at Christmastime after
all, he told himself. And maybe some Saturdays and Sundays to give him a hand. It was up to them to find a way
to move forward, if they wanted to. Then he felt the
October sun warm on his skin—don't waste it, he said to
himself, don't waste it—and he put on his boots and went
into the mountains for a hike.

Dreams of Fontana Fredda

In a room with her suitcases ready, Babette dreamed of her southern lover. He was a man who was there and wasn't, half real and half invented, but he sure knew how to do it. He was brusque with his kisses and soft with his hands. She felt free, she could ask and do whatever she wanted, and in her dream the sex made her happy, and when they did it they laughed a lot. She woke up before it finished. Why did those dreams of hers always end right at the most beautiful part? She tried to prolong it while awake and somehow succeeded, even though it wasn't the same anymore.

Santorso was in his sleep full of gin, with cold sweats and twisted guts. He dreamed of the wolf he hadn't seen yet. He was in the mountains, hunting grouse. As he followed the dog that had gone up ahead, he found the wolf in front of him, in the snow. He sat quietly, watching him. Santorso reached for his shotgun, which he would keep on his shoulder, ready to take aim at any moment, but all his hands grasped was air. Then he remembered that they had taken the gun away from him. He looked at the wolf looking at him like you look at a dotard, and said: Well, fuck me, don't I scare you? Why, I'll turn you into a fur hat! Go on now, get outta here and go back to where you came from!

Silvia, from her fifth floor on the city's outskirts, dreamed of the refuge, the glacier, and the slope that led to the Felik Pass. There was no lead in front of her. Neither Fausto nor Pasang, nor any trail that anyone had already beaten. Yet she knew the way. She went alone on that slope, planting her crampons in the icy snow, the ice ax punctuating her pace, her legs strong and sure, by now close to reaching that lost city of hers.

And that night Fausto dreamed of the old man mad about art. He could have been ninety or so. He painted on the ground, on a bamboo floor, in a room with paper walls; he could see him from the outside, but at the same time the old man was him. He was so old that he needed only three or four strokes now to paint what he had in mind. Three or four, he thought, but not one. I'll be good enough, he told himself, when I need one, to paint Fuji and all the rest. There was a daughter with him, or maybe a wife so young that she was like a daughter, who took away the finished painting and handed him a new sheet, affectionate but stern. Try again, she told him without speaking. She had long beautiful hair, black and straight and shiny and just washed.

And these dreams were part of the Fontana Fredda

landscape as much as the woods devastated by wind, the stacks of unsold logs, the dry streams of autumn, the deer that came out to graze on the ski slope not yet covered with snow, the dark houses and withered blueberries and larch trees beginning to turn yellow, the wandering sheepdogs and the thin layer of ice forming in the fountain troughs. Fontana Fredda was made in equal measure of reality and desire. And around Fontana Fredda the mountains existed, altogether indifferent to the dreams of these human beings, and would continue to exist when they woke up.

Acknowledgments

Fontane, 2021

This book is for Barbara, an artist of the refuge.
And for all my friends at the Polar Circle.

Even as a ghost,
I will keep treading lightly
through these summer woods.

A Note from the Translator

The Lovers is a deceptively simple story about sincere people. As a translator working from Italian to English, simplicity should make my task easier. Generally, certain elements of storytelling are notoriously hard to translate. Humor is one, especially humor based on word play or obscure cultural references. A more specific problem with Italian is the tendency of some authors to indulge in a tortuous exuberance akin to a Baroque church: a surfeit of adjectives and subordinate clauses, melodramatic effusions and winking ironies that, when translated into English, might strike readers as cloyingly mannered.

Fortunately for me, Paolo Cognetti is not one of those authors. In fact, Cognetti is well versed in twentieth-century American literature—particularly the "less-is-more" school popularized by Ernest Hemingway's short stories. One of these stories, "In Another Country," is mentioned by Fausto, the novel's protagonist. It's a story that hauntingly exemplifies Hemingway's "iceberg theory" of writing: namely, that most of the truth of a narrative should not be evident—rather, it should stay below the surface, working on the story invisibly, stabilizing and leavening it with the depth of its omissions.

When I first took on this project, Cognetti spoke to me about how the book had come to him, and he suggested I read Kent Haruf's *Plainsong*—another deceptively simple story about sincere people—to get a feel for the tone he had set out to achieve in Italian. He had been so struck by that novel that he wanted to create something in the same vein set in his beloved Alps. He even decided to do away with the quotation marks in the dialogues, like Haruf.

Since omissions require no effort to translate, I didn't have to worry about many of the pitfalls a literary translator encounters. My challenge was to describe the figurative iceberg reflected concretely in the novel's real protagonist: Monte Rosa and the valleys around it. The Italian Alps, unlike many other mountain ranges, have for thousands of years been distinct for the contrast they offer between their cold, inhospitable terrain and their proximity to "civilization." This dichotomy serves as the story's undertow, pulling the characters in directions that go against their will. The mountains determine the human lives that are drawn to them, and those lives are in turn humbled by nature's implacable beauty and truth—even in the terror it can unleash.

For me, the real difficulty—and pleasure—was to approximate, if not duplicate, the sheer poetry of Cognetti's poignantly spare prose. His descriptions of landscapes, of changing seasons, or of animals—whether a wolf sniffing for traces of man, or cows chased to their deaths down a ravine and left as carrion for scavengers—pierce through the reader. And the poetry moves the reader to feel why the characters need to be so sincere up there in the higher altitudes. Because nature will not suffer the illusions of humans too full of themselves.

A few specific technical issues that cropped up in this translation might be worth mentioning. Both reflect subtle cultural differences.

First, there is the word *ragazza*. It can mean a girl from puberty up to a young woman. But the use of *ragazza* for a mature woman is less determined by age than by a certain youthful quality. I tried to translate *ragazza* as "young woman" where suitable, but there were sections where using "girl"—even for the twenty-seven-year-old Silvia—seemed more appropriate. For example, in the contrast between Fausto's two women:

> The only heat in Silvia's room was what came from the kitchen, so the ritual of undressing was a bit rushed, but for Fausto, slipping into bed nude, next to an equally nude and trembling girl [*ragazza,* 27 years old], had something moving and marvelous about it. He had been with the same woman [*donna*, now pushing 40] for ten years, and for six months with his own insipid company.

In Italian, *ragazza* and *donna* often overlap. And refer-ring to a mature woman as a *ragazza* is often construed as a compliment. So, if the choice of "girl" sounds tone deaf to some, please blame the translator, not the author.

The other issue, though not as recurring, hits home at the end of the book. There are two ways of communicating "I love you" in Italian: *ti amo*, which is implicitly erotic (a mother or father could never say *"ti amo"* to their child without raising eyebrows); and *ti voglio bene* (literally, "I want good for you"), which is reserved for family and dear friends. When, at the end of the book, Silvia tells Fausto, *"Ti voglio bene,"* the standard translation should be, "I love you." But as all Italians know, when a lover chooses *"ti voglio bene"* instead of *"ti amo,"* it's clearly a hedge. It means: "I love you, but not enough to commit seriously and sacrifice my life for that love." The inher-ent let down in their exchange is lost in English. I chose to have Silvia say something very earnest: "You mean a lot to me." And Fausto echoes her. Although everyone knows—beneath the surface—what Fausto really wants to say is: "I love you."

But that's yet another challenge with this sort of story: How do you translate the power of what's left unsaid?

—Stash Luczkiw

Here ends Paolo Cognetti's
The Lovers.

The first edition of this book was printed and
bound at LSC Communications in
Harrisonburg, Virginia, March 2022.

A NOTE ON THE TYPE

The text of this novel was set in Sabon, an old-style
serif typeface created by Jan Tschichold between 1964
and 1967. Drawing inspiration from the elegant and
highly legible designs of the famed sixteenth-century
Parisian typographer and publisher Claude Garamond, the font's name honors Jacques Sabon, one of
Garamond's close collaborators. Sabon has remained
a popular typeface in print, and it is admired for its
smooth and tidy appearance.

HarperVia

An imprint dedicated to publishing international
voices, offering readers a chance to encounter
other lives and other points of view via
the language of the imagination.